"Maggie."

Matt's voice was deep. Smooth. The only sound in her world at that moment. "I think you're the center of it all and that message might have just proven it."

"How?"

She needed the truth. She needed it so badly that she moved closer to the man. On reflex she tilted her head back to meet his stare easier. Had they ever been this close before?

And was it her imagination or did he look down at her lips?

"The message," he repeated, derailing her unwelcome thoughts. "It proves that whoever wrote it either *knows* you or researched you well enough to get really personal information."

"But why? Why would I need a reminder if I know him already?"

Maggie already didn't like what he was going to say. A storm seemed to start up in his eyes. Deep eyes, drenched in mystery.

"My guess? He's saying that he doesn't just know you. He knows your past and your present." She watched as his jaw hardened. "It's a threat, Maggie. A personal one."

FORGOTTEN PIECES

—

TYLER ANNE SNELL

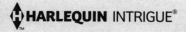
HARLEQUIN INTRIGUE®

This book is for Kortnie B. and every other ER nurse out there.

I can't imagine what you all must go through during every shift but I am immensely grateful that you do so with courage, wisdom and compassion.

You're the real superheroes.

ISBN-13: 978-1-335-52615-1

Forgotten Pieces

Copyright © 2017 by Tyler Anne Snell

Recycling programs for this product may not exist in your area.

Printed in U.S.A.

Tyler Anne Snell genuinely loves all genres of the written word. However, she's realized that she loves books filled with sexual tension and mysteries a little more than the rest. Her stories have a good dose of both. Tyler lives in Alabama with her same-named husband and their mini "lions." When she isn't reading or writing, she's playing video games and working on her blog, *Almost There*. To follow her shenanigans, visit tylerannesnell.com.

Books by Tyler Anne Snell

Harlequin Intrigue

The Protectors of Riker County

Small-Town Face-Off
The Deputy's Witness
Forgotten Pieces

Orion Security

Private Bodyguard
Full Force Fatherhood
Be on the Lookout: Bodyguard
Suspicious Activities

Manhunt

Visit the Author Profile page at Harlequin.com.

CAST OF CHARACTERS

Detective Matt Walker—After an accident takes his wife's life, this detective spends years trying to move on. It isn't until new evidence is discovered that he realizes he'll have to revisit the one case that nearly destroyed him. Can he finally find the truth about what happened to his wife all of those years ago? And can he keep a beautiful and infuriating ex-reporter out of harm's way while they search for it?

Maggie Carson—Once a rising young star in local journalism, this ex-reporter understands how quickly life can go downhill. After refusing to let go of a theory about the accidental death of Erin Walker, her life completely changes. Years later it turns out she might just have been right all along. Will she finally be able to find justice for a woman she never knew? Can she do it alongside the hot-as-hell detective who only thinks of her as the enemy?

Erin Walker—Late wife to Matt and killed by what is originally deemed as an accident, she becomes the subject of Maggie's personal investigation spanning years after her passing.

Cody Carson—Adopted son of Maggie, this young boy is one of the main reasons Maggie and Matt will do whatever it takes to finish what someone else started all those years ago.

Dwayne Meyers—Retired detective and mentor to Matt, he becomes one of the many puzzle pieces in the investigation into Erin's death.

Kortnie Bean—As an emergency-room nurse and quick friend to Maggie, she gets a firsthand look at what someone is willing to do to keep the ex-reporter quiet.

Sheriff Billy Reed—Friend and boss to Matt, he's no stranger to the dangers of a case that's personal, but that won't stop him from doing everything within his power to help solve it.

Chapter One

"What's a seven-letter word for a man who is an all-around donkey to the people who are just trying to help him?"

Maggie Carson shifted her weight to the other foot and blew a frustrated breath out. It moved a wayward spiral of hair out of her face. She tried to tuck it back into the makeshift ponytail holder but it was a no-go. Like her it was probably done with the flip-flopping, hot-and-cold weather. Humid to the point of feeling like you were swimming standing up and then nothing but a dry chill. It was like south Alabama had a fever. Not that she was overly concerned about the weather.

At least not when she was in the process of breaking and entering.

Or *attempting* to break and enter.

"Not going to answer me, huh?"

She gave the man crouched down next to her, fiddling with the lock, a look that would have done her reputation for being a handful proud. Except the man wasn't having any of it. He kept his eyes straight ahead and his fingers working.

Those fingers.

Those hands.

Oh, Lordy, what she could do with those.

Maggie shook her head, and the thought, away, surprised it had sprung up in the first place. Sure, Detective Matt Walker was a twelve on a ten-point scale of yummy—there was no denying that—but he was also still *Detective Matt Walker*. A man who had once called her a no-good ambulance chaser, pot stirrer and a scourge against society without an ounce of regret or shame. Not that she blamed him. She *had* accused him of murder. His wife's murder, to boot.

But she *had* apologized for that.

"Fine, I'll tell you," she said, bending at the waist to keep her volume low. The smell of some generic cologne wafted up to her. The image of his hands came back. Maggie powered through it. "The magic word is *jack*—"

The lock unlatched, distracting her from her insult. For now.

"Tricking me into coming over to break into your house because you got locked out isn't helping me," he deadpanned. "In fact, that's making a false report and is punishable by law." He stood tall and brushed off his jeans. "And I'd be lying if I said I hadn't fantasized about carting you off to jail before."

A smirk pulled up the corners of his lips—the bottom one plump and ripe for the taking—but Maggie knew he was telling the truth without his snark. Which was why she'd kept her distance for the past five years. Still, it seemed there might not be enough time in the world to put their particular stream of water under the bridge.

"It's not considered tricking if it's the only way I can get the lead detective to come here," she pointed out. "Also, I really did lock myself out. Two birds, one stone."

Matt crossed his arms over his chest. For what felt like a long moment but she doubted stretched past a few seconds, Maggie took stock of the changes that had happened to his appearance since their last blowout years before. His hair was still a shade of dark dirty blond but now it was shaved short on the sides while the top had more length. It was a more controlled and clean look—probably part of being one of the county's most beloved detectives—and paired like a fine wine with the dusting of facial hair he also, no doubt, kept maintained to the point where no one could ever complain that he was unkempt. Not that she'd seen him be anything but proper and in control during his career with the Riker County Sheriff's Department. She might have been trying to avoid him but that didn't mean she'd missed newspaper articles and stories of cases he was involved in on the local news.

However, in person, Maggie had to admit there were a few points that had been lost in the media's translation of the man in front of her. The first and foremost was a pair of blue-gray eyes that always carried a hawk-like intensity. She imagined if she had the time she'd still not be able to put their level of intrigue on a scale. It was like looking into a spring and feeling its chill before ever even dipping a toe in the water. Then there was that jawline. The description of *chiseled* didn't do him, or any woman caught staring at him, justice. It was so perfect that Maggie's hand was itching to run along it before stopping just below his lips. For all she cared the rest of the man could have been a stick figure and she'd still rate him at an easy eleven. But it certainly didn't hurt his cause that he was tall and had muscles peeking through his button-down. *That* was a change from the last time she'd seen him in person. He'd been more lean and less toned. Then again, she wasn't surprised.

Everyone worked through grief differently.

Some people started a new hobby; some people threw themselves into the gym.

Others investigated unsolved murders in secret.

"And why, of all people, would you need me here?" Matt asked, cutting through her mental breakdown of him.

Instead of stepping backward, utilizing the large open space of her front porch, she chanced a step forward.

"I found something," she started, straining out any excess enthusiasm that might make her seem coarse. Still, she knew the detective was a keen observer.

Which is why his frown was already doubling in on itself before she explained herself.

"I don't want to hear this," he interrupted, voice like ice. "I'm warning you, Carson."

"And it wouldn't be the first time you've done so," she countered, skipping over the fact he'd said her last name like a teacher readying to send her to detention. "But right now I'm telling you I found a lead. A *real*, honest-to-God lead!"

The detective's frown affected all of his body. It pinched his expression and pulled his posture taut. Through gritted teeth, he rumbled out his thoughts with disdain clear in his words.

"Why do you keep doing this? What gives you the right?" He took a step away from her. That didn't stop Maggie.

"It wasn't an accident," she implored. "I can prove it now."

Matt shook his head. He skipped frustrated and flew right into angry. This time Maggie faltered.

"You have no right digging into this," he growled. "You didn't even *know* Erin."

"But don't you want to hear what I found?"

Matt made a stop motion with his hands. The jaw she'd been admiring was set. Hard. "I don't want to ever talk to you again. Especially about this." He turned and was off the front porch in one fluid motion. Before he got into his truck he paused. "And next time you call me out here, I won't hesitate to arrest you."

And then he was gone.

THE RIKER COUNTY Sheriff's Department was quiet. Not that that was a bad thing but after the morning he'd had, Matt was itching to work a case. Anything to distract him from the storm of emotions raging through him. If he was being objective, he knew he'd be surprised at how one woman could affect him so completely. Then again, that woman *was* Maggie Carson. If she was good at anything it was leaving lasting impressions.

Without opening the bottom drawer, he imagined the picture within it. Erin Walker, smiling up at him. His beautiful wife. Unaware that a year later she'd be in the wrong place at the wrong time.

Matt fisted his hands on the top of his desk.

"So you're ticked off, huh?" A knock pulled his attention to the doorway and the man standing inside it. Sheriff Billy Reed wasn't frowning but he wasn't smiling, either. "I heard you answered a suspicious persons call on your way in this morning. A potential breaking and entering?"

Matt opened his hands slowly. He sighed.

Billy wasn't just his sheriff, he was also one of Matt's closest friends. There wasn't any use trying to hedge around the truth. Or flat out lie.

"The only suspicious person was the woman who called in the false report to get me there in the first place. I should have let a deputy handle it but she asked specifically for me. It was a trap," he admitted, earning an eyebrow raise from his boss, "set by Maggie Carson."

Billy's demeanor shifted to understanding. He might not have been sheriff five years ago but that didn't mean he'd missed what had happened. Or why Matt had such an issue with Maggie.

"What did she want? I thought she hasn't tried to talk to you in years."

Matt tried to keep his rising anger in check.

"She said she had a lead that proves Erin's death wasn't an accident."

Billy scowled, disapproval shrouding his expression.

"What's the lead?"

"Hell if I know. I didn't give her the chance to tell me," he admitted. "She doesn't have the best track record with me."

"I thought she would have moved on from the case," Billy said. "I wonder what it was she thought she found." Behind his words was a new curiosity. And, if Matt hadn't been so close to the situation, he would have listened to his own need to know. However, he *was* too close. And apparently, unlike Maggie, he had moved on.

"Maybe she's tired of writing magazine fluff pieces," Matt offered. "And now she's trying to claw her way back to the news spotlight by digging up the past she has no business digging up."

Billy stepped into the office. It was small and the bull pen of deputies started a few feet away. The sheriff must not have wanted them to hear what he was about to say, though. He lowered his voice.

"But what about the anonymous tip we got six months ago? Maybe it wouldn't hurt to hear her out?"

Matt started to bristle. He'd been completely blind-sided when he'd received a call from a man who claimed the same thing Maggie had. That the car accident that had killed Erin and one other pedestrian, hadn't been an accident at all. At the time the anonymous caller refused to identify himself unless Matt drove to Georgia to meet him. He'd only told Billy and the chief deputy, Suzy Simmons. They'd gone to the meet location together, only to find a note left with a waitress that read "I'm sorry." Matt and Suzy had stuck around to try to track down the man but they hadn't had any luck.

"That man could have been unstable or bored or both," he said. "For all we know Maggie could have orchestrated the whole thing." Even as he said it, Matt doubted his words. Whatever his issues with Maggie, he didn't think she was that malicious. He let out another long breath. "I just—I've finally gotten to a good place with what happened to Erin," Matt admitted. "And until I find some hard evidence that the accident that killed my wife wasn't an accident at all, then I'd prefer to not start up and drag another investigation along."

Billy nodded.

"And I don't blame you for that," he said. "If Maggie gives you any more trouble, let me know." He cracked a smile and tapped the badge on his belt. "I'm not afraid to use this thing."

Matt thanked him and spent the rest of the day avoiding any and all thoughts of Maggie, anonymous tips that led nowhere and an investigation he had drowned himself in years before. It wasn't until he had left the department and was driving home in the setting sun that he didn't have to distract himself from his thoughts. Instead, when his phone rang and the caller ID read "Dwayne," Matt felt his lips pull up into a genuine smile. It had been months since he'd talked to the retired detective and, if he was being honest, his mentor.

"Well, it's been a hot minute," Matt answered, forgoing any formal greeting. He'd once spent an entire week fishing with the man. Any need for formalities between them had sunk to the bottom of the river along with the faulty lures Matt had purchased. "How've you—"

"Don't," someone yelled. But it wasn't Dwayne and it wasn't into the phone. Instead, it was in the background. And it was a woman. "Don't do it!" A scream tore through the airwaves and, even though Matt couldn't tell who it was, he made a hard U-turn.

"Dwayne?" he yelled into the phone. "Dwayne!"

A *thud* that made Matt's stomach go cold preceded the phone call ending.

Matt called the number back. It went straight to voice mail. His car filled with obscenities in between calling dispatch and navigating to the outskirts of the city of Kipsy, right in the middle of the department's jurisdiction. Matt had been to the former detective's

house on more than one occasion so when he pulled
up and cut his engine, he knew outside the phone call
that something was really wrong.

The screened-in front porch—a point of pride from
the man, so mosquitos couldn't eat him up while he
enjoyed a beer or two—was left open, the door to it
off its hinges. The wicker furniture was scattered
around the space. Nothing else on the outside looked
disturbed but what he'd seen was enough.

Without waiting for backup, Matt got out of his car
as quietly as he could. If he hadn't heard the woman
scream he might have been more cautious. But he
had. Which meant his gun came out and his attention turned to the house.

A small SUV he didn't recognize was parked at
the side but Dwayne's truck was nowhere to be seen.
Lights were on inside the house but as Matt got closer,
he didn't hear any voices or movement. The darkness
of night had fallen around him, offering cover, but
it also might give an assailant the same advantage.
It was a thought that made him slow as he got to the
front door. It was cracked open. Something Dwayne
would never do.

Matt held his gun high and pushed the door the
rest of the way open, adrenaline spiking and ready
to confront whatever had gone wrong.

Or so he thought.

"What the hell?"

The room looked like a tornado had torn through
it. Furniture was overturned, books and trinkets were

scattered and, with a drop of his gut, Matt realized blood was smeared across parts of the hardwood floor. Which shouldn't have been surprising, considering Dwayne was lying in the middle of the room, beaten badly, bloodied and unmoving.

What Matt couldn't have prepared himself for was the body next to Dwayne's.

It was Maggie. She was holding a bat covered in blood in one hand while a folder was next to the other. Matt felt like he was dreaming as his eyes focused on the name written across the top of it.

It was *his* name.

Chapter Two

It was her college graduation party all over again. Or, rather, the aftermath of it. Maggie's head was pounding. Worse than the hangover she'd had after her roommate, Barb, had decided bringing cake-flavored vodka was a good idea. While it had been a hit at the time, Maggie had felt like she was the one who had been hit the next day.

Which was how she felt as she sat on a hospital bed, staring at an IV in one arm and a pair of hand-cuffs around her other wrist. It connected her to the hospital bed and, according to a deputy she didn't know, had been an order. It was one of many things that had confused her since she'd come to in an ambulance, staring up at a woman asking her what her name was and if she could hear her.

While Maggie knew the hospital staff was doing all they could to make sure she was getting the treat-ment she needed, they sure as heck hadn't bothered to fill her in on a few details. Like why she'd wound up in an ambulance to begin with, where she had been before the ambulance had been called and why she was barefoot. That last detail, of all things, irrationally bothered her more than the rest. Because, much like the aftermath of her graduation party, she seemed to be missing a chunk of memory. This time, though, she hadn't the faintest idea what had prompted it.

A knock sounded on the door before a nurse pushed it open.

"How are you doing, Ms. Carson?"

A redheaded woman with bold lipstick and an easy smile slid into the room. When her gaze went to the handcuffs that smile tightened. Maggie decided to address the obvious.

"I'd really like to not be handcuffed," she said. "And to not be in the hospital. Neither were on my to-do list today. Or, at least I don't remember them if they were."

The nurse gravitated over to the IV.

"The cuffs I can't help," she admitted. "But what I can do is ask how your head is feeling. So, Ms. Carson, how is your head?" She met Maggie's stare. It was a look that was equal parts concerned and authoritative. She was trying to do her job and Maggie was being snarky. She sighed.

"There are few people in this world who ever use my last name and usually it's when they're about to yell at me. So, please, call me Maggie. But on the head-hurting front, it's throbbing. Not as bad as before, but it's there."

The nurse looked at Maggie's chart.

"And you're still having trouble with recall?"

Maggie nodded. It hurt.

"I'm also having trouble understanding why my head hurts in the first place." Maggie lowered her voice, trying to convey something she often tried to hide. Vulnerability. "Because no one, and I mean no one, has told me what happened to me since I woke up in an ambulance with my shirt and bra cut open and monitors stuck to my chest. So, please—" Maggie glanced down at the woman's name tag "—Nurse Bean, give me *something*."

For a moment the nurse looked like she was going to shake her head and try to offer another polite smile. Instead, she surprised Maggie by answering.

"To be honest, I just started my shift so I don't know all of the details. What I do know is that you being knocked out wasn't an accident." Her lips thinned. "But as for who did it, why and where... I'm sorry. Those are questions I can't answer."

Maggie's stomach turned cold. She knew she shouldn't have been surprised that she had been attacked since it wasn't every day she lost hours of memory, but having a nurse say it aloud was on the surreal side of uncomfortable.

"Well, I guess I'm glad to know I didn't wind up this way after tripping and bumping my head or anything," Maggie deadpanned. Sarcasm was her safety blanket. The throbbing from her head now made a fraction of sense. That in itself should have been comforting. But it wasn't. "Thank you for leveling with me," she added on. "I don't want to say I'm scared but, well, it's not a good feeling to be me right now. Thanks."

The nurse gave a quick nod and smile of acceptance.

"Like you, I prefer to go by my first name. So call me Kortnie." She took the chart and started to turn away. "I'll be back in a few minutes to check on you."

Maggie was ready to let her go and wait for someone who did know the inside scoop but then the cold steel of the handcuffs against her skin brought her attention to one more question.

"You have to at least know why I'm handcuffed, right?"

Kortnie's smile faltered.

"That's a question you should ask Detective Walker."

"Is he going to make it?"

Matt roused from the large square tile he'd been standing on for what felt like hours. It was outside Dwayne's room and was better than standing and staring inside it. Matt didn't like hospitals. Or, really, he didn't like the helplessness that came with them. He couldn't help Dwayne in his current condition. He couldn't make him heal any faster. He couldn't make him survive. All he could do was help from where he hovered and tried to puzzle out what had happened the night before. Not that he'd had much success in that department.

The sheriff repeated his question with an added inflection of empathy. He wasn't as close to the retired detective as Matt but he knew him well enough to grab the occasional drink or watch a football game or two together.

"He's out of the immediate woods but his injuries are extensive," Matt answered, dragging a hand down his face. "He still hasn't woken up and, if I read the doc's body language correctly, there's a good chance he might not. Or, if he does, he might not be the same Dwayne we knew. There was some bleeding on the brain." Billy cursed beneath his breath. Matt let him finish before he continued, "So unless the crime scene yielded some incredible results, our only way of knowing what happened might be down there. And, like I told you on the phone last night, according to *her* doctor she's having short-term memory issues."

He pointed in the direction of Maggie Carson's room. She'd been transferred out of the ER a few hours ago.

The sheriff followed his finger.

"Have you talked to her yet?" Billy asked.

Matt shook his head. Frustration, anger and more frustration sprang up at just the thought of the woman.

"When we first came in I stuck with Dwayne," he admitted. "By the time he was stable and put in his room, she was getting CAT scans. Then she was out, thanks to some pain meds. I was going to wait until the morning to talk to her." Matt really took in the sheriff's appearance. He couldn't help but smirk. "And considering there's applesauce on your blazer, I'm assuming it's morning."

Billy looked down at the smudge and sighed but in no way seemed angry.

"What can I say? Alexa and I have a routine. She wakes up early and we negotiate how much applesauce she's going to eat." He motioned to the stain. "It's a messy business. I've dealt with seasoned criminals that were easier to crack than this toddler."

There was pride clear and true in the way Billy spoke of his daughter. It matched his unconditional love for his wife, Mara. Which was one of the reasons so many residents of Riker County took a shine to him. He was a good family man who worked hard to provide and protect. He was the straightest shooter Matt had ever known in law enforcement. Something that had not always been the case for everyone he had employed.

Matt watched as Billy sobered.

"I would tell you that going home to get some sleep might be the best course for you and that I can handle talking to Maggie," he started. "But—"

"It's Dwayne that got hurt and I won't back off yet."

Billy nodded.

"Then let's go talk to Maggie."

They marched down the hallway and knocked on the door. Matt spied the clock on the wall. Hours had indeed passed. It was almost seven in the morning.

"Come in!"

Matt took his attempt at a calming breath and followed the sheriff inside.

If he thought they'd be met with guilt or shame, he was wildly mistaken.

One look at him, and Maggie's big green eyes got bigger. Her lips didn't have time to purse. They were too busy parting to yell at him.

"I know you have your issues with me, but *this* is ridiculous, don't you think?"

She shook her left arm.

Matt walked to the side of the bed as if he was going to inspect the cuffs. Instead, he crossed his arms over his chest.

"Considering the nature of what happened, we deemed it necessary."

Maggie looked like a fish out of water, opening and closing her mouth, trying to find the right words to fight him with, no doubt. Billy, however, stepped in. He closed the door behind them and cleared his throat.

"Let's calm down and talk," he said.

"Can we talk about how I've been cuffed to a bed for the entire night and no one, until now, has decided to come and talk to me other than doctors?"

Maggie's cheeks were flushed, Matt noticed. For the first time he realized there was a light dusting of freckles across her nose.

"Yes," Billy said, channeling the calm that Matt

had heard him use throughout their careers. "But first, tell us the last thing you remember."

Maggie let out a breath of frustration.

"Sneaking off to my couch in the middle of the night because I couldn't sleep. I channel surfed until I fell asleep in front of the TV."

Matt shared a look with Billy.

"In the middle of the night," Billy repeated. "And by *night* you mean…"

Maggie sighed.

"By *night* I mean Tuesday night." She held up her hand in a stopping motion. "And, before you question my sanity, yes, I know that today is Thursday."

"You're missing more than twenty-four hours," Billy spelled out. Maggie nodded. Matt noticed she was more inclined to look at the sheriff with controlled emotions. When she looked at him, he could see the fire burning behind her eyes. Not that he could blame her. The phrase "poking the bear" came to mind. Not that Maggie Carson in any way looked like a bear.

"So you don't remember your conversation with Detective Walker yesterday?" Billy added on.

Maggie's eyes widened.

"No?" Her eyebrow rose as she looked at Matt for an explanation.

He didn't want to give it. He was too frustrated.

"Well, isn't that convenient?" Matt muttered.

Forgotten Pieces

The comment didn't go unnoticed. Maggie whipped her head around to Billy and then back to Matt.

"Hey, what's that supposed to mean? Do you think I'm making this up? Why would I even do that?"

"Oh, I don't know, covering your a—"

"Detective," Billy interrupted, voice sharp. Matt felt anger surge again. If he was honest, it was misplaced. While he did have issues with Maggie Carson, he had never pegged her for a violent woman. Aggressive with her words, sure. Stubborn to the point where he really had fantasized about arresting her a few times, absolutely. But was she capable of beating a man in his sixties to the point of potential brain damage? No. He felt it in his gut, whether or not he wanted to absolve her of the accusation that she'd done it.

Still, the only witnesses that they knew of were both in the hospital. One might never wake up. The other was claiming memory loss. That was a tough pill to swallow no matter who the two were.

"I'm sure the doctor would be happy to talk to you about it." Maggie cooled down as she spoke to Billy. "But I would like to know why you thought I would make it up."

She kept her eyes firmly on Billy. He squared his shoulders.

"What's your relationship with Dwayne Meyers?"

Matt watched closely as Maggie's expression turned to confusion. Her eyebrows drew together. She tilted her head ever so slightly to the side.

"I wouldn't say we have one," she answered. "I mean, we know each other and I've interviewed him before. But other than that I don't think you could even classify us as friends. Why do you ask?"

"Because I found you at his house," Matt said.

Again Maggie tilted her head to the side. Like the movement would shake loose a memory that would make the puzzle whole. Then her face lit up.

"Well, then, did he tell you who did this to me?" She motioned to the back of her head where the initial blow that had knocked her unconscious had happened. While waiting for the ambulance Matt had inspected the injury in an attempt to understand the situation a little better. It hadn't helped. "Unless... Did *he* do this to me?"

"That's what we're trying to piece together," Billy hedged.

"Why not ask Dwayne?"

Matt took another step forward. He knew Billy was trying to ease the woman into the information to see how she reacted but Matt was tired of it. Tired in general. It was time to cut to the chase.

"Because you weren't the only one I found," he started. "Dwayne was beaten badly with, as far as we can guess, a baseball bat. One that you were holding when I found you."

A crinkle began to deepen between Maggie's eyebrows. She took a moment to respond with notable reserve.

"You think someone attacked us both and left the bat behind?"

"Or it was you who attacked Dwayne," Matt offered.

That crease turned from concern to something he couldn't read. It caught Matt off guard.

"I might not remember an entire day or so, but I wouldn't hurt Dwayne Meyers. In fact, I wouldn't *use a bat* to hurt anyone unless it was self-defense," she said, voice even. "And, even if I had, what do you think happened? You think I used him as batting practice and then knocked myself unconscious? What would I gain from any of that?" This time her eyes found Matt's and hunkered down on them. "I know you don't like me but do you really think I'm capable of that?"

Matt remembered the first time he'd seen Maggie Carson. Her thick, wavy hair had been short then, but still wild. Despite five years it was the same dark oak color with a few new spots of lightened brown from, he guessed, days spent outside in the sun. She was still slender, as she had been back then, but not as rigid. When she'd first introduced herself Matt remembered thinking she looked very much like a woman with the world on her shoulders, forced to struggle to keep them upright. He'd never stopped to think about the woman's personal life much past that, considering she had been there to question him about Erin's death. But now?

Matt caught himself wondering about the life of

the woman staring up at him with true, forest green eyes. Ones he realized he'd never really forgotten.

Ones he realized he believed.

But then what had gone on in that house?

Chapter Three

Matt opened his mouth to answer Maggie's question when a knock on the door interrupted his thoughts. The three of them turned just as it was opened.

A young woman, maybe early twenties, flushed at the sight of them.

"Oh, I—I'm sorry," she said hurriedly, eyes bouncing across each of their faces. "The nurse said you were awake and we could come back."

No sooner than she'd said the word *we* did a boy with round glasses pop his head around her hip. His gaze went straight to Maggie's.

Out of Matt's periphery he saw her entire demeanor change.

"Well, hey there, little dude," she exclaimed, voice softening.

The boy, perhaps five or six, beamed. Then, just as quickly, he shrank back and looked up at the men. He was shy.

"It's okay," Maggie coaxed. "These are Mommy's friends."

Mommy? Matt thought, surprised. He hadn't known she had a kid.

"We can come back," the younger woman blurted out, face now completely red. Her gaze shifted to Maggie again and then dropped down to what must have been her wrist cuffed to the railing. "I—I can skip class today," she offered.

Matt took a step to his right until he was touching the bed. It effectively cut off everyone's view of the cuffs.

Billy cleared his throat.

"I don't think we've met," he said, stepping forward with his hand outstretched. He moved into the woman's and child's sightlines, also blocking Maggie from view. "I'm Sheriff Billy Reed."

Matt turned, pulling his handcuff key out. Maggie remained silent as she watched him uncuff her as quietly as he could. She met his gaze and gave one small nod.

A silent thank-you.

It, like the boy, caught him off guard.

He returned it with a nod of his own.

Like she said, he might have issues with her, but he wasn't heartless. The boy was probably already freaked out that his mother was in the hospital.

But where was his dad?

Matt turned back to the sheriff and his conversation, trying to move past thoughts of Maggie's love life. He had bigger things to worry about.

"I'm Larissa. I babysit Cody occasionally."

"So then, you must be Cody," Billy said. Matt watched him kneel down in front of the boy. He nodded. "And I'm guessing you are ready to hang out with your mom for a bit." Again the boy nodded. "Well, why don't I make you a deal? You go grab a quick hug from her and then you can walk with me to the vending machine down the hall for an early-morning candy bar while my friend Matt finishes talking to your mom." Matt didn't have to be next to Cody to see his face light up at the mention of a candy bar. Billy turned to Maggie. "If that's okay with you?"

"Only if you save half of it for me," she said with a grin. Another expression Matt wasn't used to seeing from the woman.

Cody nodded, raced forward and jumped on the bed for a hug. Maggie winced but kept smiling. Even with the meds she was being fed there must have still been some pain from the hit that had knocked her out. She returned the hug with a few words in the boy's ear Matt couldn't hear. He giggled and then was off with the sheriff. Larissa followed, still flushed.

"If you needed a reason to believe I didn't attack Dwayne, then that boy is it," Maggie started. "I don't need to be able to remember the last day to tell you with certainty that I wouldn't jeopardize his life by suddenly being a violent and callous woman."

"Then give me a reason why you *were* at Dwayne's," Matt said. "Because I can't accept that everything that happened in the last day came out of nowhere. If you weren't friendly with the man, then you must have been talking to him about something."

That crease between Maggie's eyebrows came back in force. Her eyes unfocused and her normally plump lips thinned. She was thinking. About what, though, he'd pay good money to be in on.

"I have had no reason to talk to Dwayne in years," she finally said. "Whatever the reason was, it must have happened yesterday." Matt was about to open his mouth and vent his frustration when Maggie continued. This time, however, there was a different tone to her words. "*But* the last time I talked to him, years ago…"

Her gaze slid up to his. Slow. Almost sheepish.

Matt didn't have to be a detective to figure out what she was trying to say.

"The last time you talked to him was after my wife died," he inserted. Even as he said it the old ache of loss sounded in the distance. "And then yesterday you tried to tell me you could prove Erin's death wasn't an accident."

He read surprise clearly on the woman's face. If she was faking it, she was doing a damned good job.

"Let me guess, another thing you don't remember." Maggie shook her head.

"No but yes," she said. "I *was* looking into the accident again but I definitely didn't have any proof."

Maggie sat up straighter. Again her gaze found his. Even with her makeup washed off, there was an almost-open kind of beauty about her. Like she had nothing to hide. But he knew better. Not only did she have something to hide, she'd also hidden it well from him for years.

"Matt," she started, unblinking. "I know you have a hard time believing this but I think I might have figured out who killed your wife."

"I'M GOING TO release you from custody for a few different reasons and with a condition or two."

Sheriff Reed had his arms crossed over his chest but didn't look like he was being pained to talk to her. Unlike the detective. After she'd dropped her bombshell, she'd more than expected him to give her a weighty, anger-filled lecture. Instead, he'd excused himself and gone into the hallway. Now she was staring at the sheriff, wondering if he knew what she'd admitted to the detective.

"Okay, I'm listening," she added when she realized Sheriff Reed wanted a confirmation.

He held up his index finger and ticked off his points as he made them.

"One, where you were struck with the baseball bat suggests that someone swung and hit you from behind." He held up his other hand to stop her questions and continued, "Based on the angle of the wound, it would have been nearly impossible for you to have been able to hit that spot with enough force to knock yourself out cold. Which means we're looking for a third person who was in that house. Detective Ansler is on scene and CSU will get back to us when they find something. For all we know you walked in on a robbery in progress. Two, your doctor has cleared you health-wise so I don't see a reason to force you to stay in one of these rooms when I know exactly where you live. And some of your neighbors, too. Including a very observant Deputy Carrington." There was a warning beneath the words. Or maybe it was a promise. It was the sheriff's way of flexing his connection muscles.

Basically he was saying, "Don't try to run or do anything stupid because I have eyes and ears almost everywhere in town."

But Maggie had no reason to run. However, doing something stupid was an entirely different ballgame. She preferred the phrase "risk taking."

"Three," he continued, holding up three fingers. "As much as I dislike the digging that you've done into the life and pain of Detective Walker, it's highly likely that the circumstances surrounding your and Dwayne's attack could be related to you digging into Erin's death and not just random. That's too much of a coincidence for me to ignore. I want to see what information you *do* have on the case. And why someone might want that information, if that's what they were after." Sheriff Reed sobered. "But you *will not* continue to look into Erin's death, understood?"

Maggie liked to think she could read people. Or at least, know what they *really* meant when they said something. That was how she knew that the sheriff meant every word of the command. And there was nothing she could say to him in that moment to convince him otherwise. So she decided to lose this battle.

But not the war.

"Understood."

Sheriff Reed nodded. His shoulders loosened considerably.

"And the last reason is your son, Cody," he said. "I hadn't realized his father wasn't in—"

"He doesn't have a father," Maggie interrupted so quickly she surprised herself. The sheriff amended his statement.

"I hadn't realized you were a single parent with no immediate family in the area who he could stay with until this is all figured out. A hospital is no place for a kid to hang out unless absolutely necessary."

"Normally, I'd agree," Maggie said after a moment. "But if my being at Dwayne's was because I was *investigating*, then what if that third person in Dwayne's house decides to come after me? Surely I've seen their face. Cody will be in danger."

"Which brings me to my two conditions," he said. "I want you to keep to your normal routine, including his, until we have this sorted out. Send your son to school today. I know what it's like to disrupt a kid's routine when they're young. He'll be safe there and in the meantime we can make sure your house is safe just in case. I would also like you to not talk about what happened to you until we have a better handle on the situation. That includes the media…

And no personal reporting of any kind. This story, you need to keep under wraps. It'll be a whole hell of a lot easier getting information when we don't have to sift through a county's worth of theories on what happened. Not yet at least."

"Okay, I can do that, I guess," she said. Though she could feel the prickling sensation of curiosity trying to expand within her. She wanted to hit the street, ask questions and get answers about what had happened to her. What had she found? How did Dwayne fit in? Or maybe she'd simply been in the wrong place at the wrong time. Still, that left the question of who had attacked them. One she wanted answered, even if it had nothing to do with her personal investigation. Plus, the sheriff was probably right. Lying low might be the best thing for her. Maybe her memories would return if she took it easy.

Ha. Easy. Like I've ever done what's easy.

Before the sheriff could read any mischief in her expression, Maggie sat up straighter and cleared her throat.

"So what's the last condition?" she asked. "Because I'd really like to leave this charming place as soon as possible."

The sheriff definitely wasn't smirking anymore. In fact, he almost looked hesitant.

"What happened could have been a case of you seeing something you shouldn't have by accident, caught as an innocent bystander and targeted for that reason. But we have no proof. Just as we have no proof that your life could be in danger. So for the public's safety and your own, I am relinquishing you into the custody of Detective Matt Walker effective immediately."

Maggie opened her mouth to argue but the sheriff was faster on the draw.

"Until we find out what happened in that house, Ms. Carson, this decision is final. Arguing with me won't work."

Maggie lifted her chin a fraction. She crossed her arms over her chest.

"No offense, Sheriff, but you've never heard me argue before."

Chapter Four

There were a lot of questions but not many answers.
At least none that led Matt to a clear picture of what
had happened at Dwayne's house. Although Maggie
had admitted to looking into Erin's accident, she'd
gone tight-lipped as they left the hospital. Then
again, that might have had more to do with Cody
being caught between them as they got into Matt's
off-duty, dark green Jimmy. The six-year-old had
kept his eyes wide as Maggie talked to him in the
back seat. She reminded him of a lesson she'd already taught him.

Don't talk to strangers.

In the rearview mirror Matt could see the boy took
the conversation seriously. He watched Maggie with
concentration that furrowed his brow. When she was
done that concentration turned to worry. He didn't understand what had changed. From what they'd pieced
together from Billy talking to Larissa before she left
for the community college was that everything had
been normal the day before.

Larissa lived near Cody's school and often picked him up and watched him until Maggie was done with work between four and five. Around four thirty Maggie had texted and asked if she could watch the boy until eight. After that she'd called from the hospital. Larissa had offered to keep him for the night. She hadn't told Cody why the impromptu sleepover had happened.

And now, sitting in the back seat, Matt could almost see the boy trying to figure out what had changed their normal routines to include a last-minute stay with his babysitter, a trip to the hospital and a talk about strangers.

Maggie must have sensed it, too. Matt glanced into the mirror in time to see her press her thumb between his eyebrows. She rubbed the crease gently and smiled.

"Wrinkles are for me, not you," she said. "Don't worry, little dude. Everything's going to be okay. I promise." Her voice had gone gentle, maternal strength backing up each word. It was such a contrast from the woman he knew that it surprised a smile out of him. Thankfully she didn't see it. "And if *you* promise not to worry, I'll see what I can do about taking you, Josh and Emily to the science museum in Kipsy sometime soon."

Matt didn't have to see the boy's face to know Maggie had just hit negotiation gold. A quick intake of breath from him was followed by a bigger smile reflected on his mom.

"I can show Emily the tornado ride," Cody exclaimed. "And we can play with the burp machine!"

"And don't forget the puzzle room," Maggie added on.

Cody squealed and launched into his favorite things he'd done the last time they'd been there. Along with the tornado ride, burp machine and puzzle room, he'd had fun in the music house where the floor was a keyboard. Judging by the quick sigh Maggie let out, she had *not* been a fan of the music house.

She caught Matt's eye and shook her head.

"That place is the devil," she supplied, in no way stopping the boy's conversation. He stared out the window, still counting off the different rides, exhibits and interactive experiments the museum had. "Imagine a marching band forced into one room and each one is playing a different, horribly out-of-sync tune. I'd rather take another bat to the head."

Despite himself, Matt almost smiled.

The pleasantries ended after they got to the school. Matt talked to the principal about keeping an eye out for anything or anyone suspicious, just in case, while Maggie sweet-talked the boy's teacher into dropping the mark against him being late. Or intimidated the teacher. Matt didn't know. The Maggie he'd met years ago was starting to look like a different Maggie now.

When they rendezvoused back at the Jimmy, however, it was all business. Another surprise, considering Maggie had been the one to start it.

"Okay, we need to retrace my steps from yesterday." She jumped in and buckled her seat belt but gazed straight ahead. "Let's start at my house and see what we can find there."

"You may have been released into my custody but that doesn't give you the right to issue orders," he reminded her. Though he agreed with her idea. He navigated out of the parking lot and pointed the SUV in the same direction he'd headed the day before.

"Sorry, I just assumed you'd want to figure out what happened," she said. The gentleness she'd used with her son had definitely gone to school with him. "I didn't realize you had something better to do."

Matt muttered some bad things beneath his breath. All of which Maggie didn't comment on. She was a smart woman. She knew which buttons to press. And when to stop pressing them altogether.

Or, at least, he thought she had. The fact that she was still trying to make something of Erin's death proved otherwise.

"So what do we know so far?" she said when he'd found a more peaceful state of mind. "Has CSU found anything helpful at Dwayne's house yet?"

Matt didn't like that he shook his head.

"Detective Ansler is supposed to update me when he gets more information on the prints found at the scene but I *do* know that a partial was found that didn't belong to you or Dwayne. Other than that, nothing of interest has been reported so far. You could tell a struggle had taken place but other than that I didn't have a chance to really investigate. I rode with Dwayne to the hospital when the EMTs got there. The sheriff and Ansler took over."

"Then why don't we go now?" Maggie asked, sitting up straighter.

"You want to go back to the scene of a crime where you're one of the suspects?" he had to ask. "That definitely isn't going to fly."

"I'm also one of the *victims*," she argued. "And how are we supposed to figure out what happened if you just admitted you didn't even have enough time to *really* look at the house? Plus, maybe something will jog my memory!"

It was a good idea, he had to admit, but he'd been burned by Maggie Carson's enthusiasm one too many times.

"How about you just leave the police work to the police? Despite the thoughts that I'm sure fill your head, last I checked you weren't law enforcement. In fact, last time I checked, you weren't even a reporter."

Maggie bristled. Her lips thinned. The air in the SUV seemed to go arctic.

And just like that Matt found a way to shut Maggie Carson up.

THE HOUSE AT the end of Birchwood Drive had a yellow door that stood out like a sunflower among a bucket of weeds. The moment they turned on the street, her eye was drawn to the door like there was a bull's-eye painted across the front. It made Maggie feel a touch of warmth just looking at it.

Because man, had she fought tooth and nail with the homeowners association about it.

The memory of fighting for something, even as small as the color of a door, made the detective's words' sting lessen. But not enough to press him further about going to Dwayne's. Instead, she decided to focus on another mystery.

Like what she had done after taking Cody to school the day before.

Her thoughts stalled when she realized something she hadn't even thought about until the house was right in front of her.

"The sheriff said my car was at Dwayne's but empty," she said when he cut the engine in the driveway.

"Yeah?"

"Including my purse, which also wasn't in the house."

Matt nodded.

For the first time that day Maggie let her shoulders sag.

"So along with my car key, it's safe to assume my house key is no longer in my possession." Matt turned to the front door. He hadn't thought about that detail, either. Maggie sighed. "You said you picked my lock yesterday morning? Another event I can't remember. Think you could put on a repeat performance?"

The detective led the way to the backyard and to

the back door with notable tension lining his shoulders. He kept his left arm tucked close to his stomach. Ready to unholster his gun, she bet. Something she might have deemed unnecessary under different circumstances.

"Give me a heads-up before you crack the lock," she said at his elbow as they walked up the steps. "I might not remember what I did yesterday but I never leave the house without setting the alarm. I'll need to run to the front door and disarm it once the door is—" Maggie watched, confused, as Matt opened the back door with no problems.

"Do you normally leave your doors unlocked?"

Maggie didn't answer right away. She was listening for what should have been a familiar sound.

"Not on purpose," she finally said. "But again, I always turn on the alarm before I leave. Or at least I thought I did." She motioned to the house and met the detective's eyes. "The alarm beeps until you disarm it and—"

"And there's no beeping," he finished, turning back to the open door. He unholstered his gun. "Anyone else live here?"

"No. Just me and Cody."

"Anyone else have the code?"

"Only Larissa but she has classes until two today."

Matt gave one curt nod followed by an equally curt order.

"Stay here."

"Yes, sir."

She moved to the side of the doorway as Matt held out his gun and went inside. Despite his order and her common sense, Maggie wanted to follow him. She wasn't a stranger to taking risks, though admittedly she had taken a good deal less of them since Cody had arrived, but leaving the door unlocked *and* the alarm off? That didn't sound like her. Not even memory-less her. Something must have made her leave in a hurry.

Or someone.

That thought was the glue that kept her feet in place while the detective spent the next few minutes going through the house. During that time she revolved through question after question in her head. No matter which mystery popped up about her blank yesterday, she never reached any memories. No leads. No answers.

"No one's in here," Matt said, reappearing in the doorway. His eyes found hers with a notable amount of suspicion. If it was directed at her she didn't know. "Nothing jumped out at me that might shed some light on everything but then again, this isn't my place. I don't know what to look for."

They walked into the house, both uneasy. Maggie felt her defenses—and sarcasm—rising. In the past few years her social life had declined. The people who frequented her house were few and far between. Not that she was unhappy with her life. She just wondered what conclusions the man had drawn from his pass-through.

He followed her as she went clockwise through the house, starting at the kitchen and ending in the living room. It was the heart of their home and most lived-in. Stranded toys mingled with books and blankets and other odds and ends that never seemed to get sorted to their rightful places outside the room.

The detective stood sentry next to one of the large windows at the front of the house. His gun was back in its holster but his hands hung at his sides, ready to do whatever was necessary.

Maggie took a moment to watch the man. She'd be lying if she said she hadn't thought about him off and on throughout the years. Mostly when a case he was working crossed over the media airwaves. She might have switched from a reporter to a magazine writer but that didn't mean she'd stopped reading the paper. But there had been moments, quiet moments, where the detective had crossed her mind without her conscious volition.

He'd just be there. Like he was now.

A man she barely knew.

A man who loathed her.

A man seemingly always in sync with the world.

Except when it came to her.

Maggie cleared her throat. She wasn't about to give herself permission to think about the detective as anything but a pain in her side. No. She wasn't allowed.

"Okay, so as far as I can tell the house is how I would normally leave it."

"Other than the unlocked door and the disabled alarm," Matt supplied.

"Yeah, except those. Everything else, though, looks like it did before the memory loss." To prove her point further, she turned to the couch. "See, my pillow from the other night is still there—"

Maggie's eyes caught on to a few details she'd missed. The strangeness of what she was seeing must have shown in her expression. The detective's body language became more open. He faced her with a look split between curiosity and concern.

"What is it?"

Maggie walked to the coffee table and paused. She pointed to the contents on its wooden top.

"Those are my keys," she said, thoroughly confused. "My house and car keys." She started to pick them up as if the physical contact would somehow answer the questions starting to spring up in her head when she noticed something else between the table and the couch. "And this is my purse."

"What?"

Maggie picked up her bag. She pulled out her wallet and flipped it open. Her ID, credit cards and money were inside. The same as she remembered it from before her memory blanked out.

"Everything's here."

It was a statement but even to her ears, her confusion was still running rampant. The half-filled cup of coffee with lipstick marks on its edge didn't help.

"You may think I'm a lot of things but let me tell you, messy isn't one of them."

"But you *and* your car were at Dwayne's," Matt added. "How did the keys end up back here?"

Like someone had flipped a switch, a new theory blazed across Maggie's mind. She turned around and walked straight to the kitchen. Matt's boots were heavy against the hardwood as he followed.

"Do you remember something?"

Maggie rounded the breakfast bar and made a beeline for the three metal canisters on the counter next to the sink. The one labeled Flour was open, its lid next to it. She was sure of what she *wouldn't* find within it but still had to look. After she did she turned, confused.

"It's gone."

"What's gone?"

"The spare key to my car." She motioned to the canister. "I kept it in there."

Matt looked between her and the tin for a moment.

"So let's assume you used your spare car key to drive your car to Dwayne's," he said. "Why would you need it when your original car key is in the other room? And why not take your purse?"

"Why leave a half-filled cup of coffee out? Why leave the back door unlocked and not the front? And why not set the alarm?"

Matt's eyes widened. Like her, his switch had flipped.

"Because you needed to leave in a hurry," he guessed. "But why not grab your things?"

Maggie walked to the door that opened into the kitchen. From where she stood she couldn't see the living room. But she *could* see the back door.

"I'm not one to make baseless guesses, despite your personal opinion of me, but I think someone was with me here yesterday," she started. A knot of cold began to form in her stomach. "And whoever they were must have said or done something I really didn't like."

Chapter Five

"It's a theory," Matt reminded the sheriff. He was standing in the living room, phone to his ear, and looking down at Maggie's key ring. After she'd become convinced of what had happened, he'd had to reel her in a bit. She'd excused herself to shower, not that he blamed her with dried blood caked on her head and a hospital stay that had extended through the night. Now he was bringing Billy up to speed. "But I have to agree it may be right on the money. I mean it looks like she just got up and got out. It's not adding up."

"Then we must not have the right numbers," Billy said. The background noise of the department filtered through the phone. It reminded Matt that he hadn't been home since he left for work yesterday. "I'll keep things going on my end while Ansler runs point on the investigation."

"You're giving lead to Ryan?" Matt asked, surprised. He was head detective in the sheriff's department and had been employed with them for four years longer than Ryan Ansler. Not to say that Matt didn't like the man. He was just more invested in figuring out what had happened thanks to his friendship with Dwayne. Which, he realized two seconds too late, might have been the problem.

"You need to figure out Ms. Carson's part in all of this," Billy said. "Whether or not she was in the wrong place at the wrong time, at the right place at the wrong time, or did exactly what she wanted to do. Finding out what happened with her is the key to solving this case. Trying to juggle everything at the same time won't help Dwayne. Getting answers about what happened at that house might. Let Ansler and me cover the other details and questions. You focus on Carson."

Billy was right. Like always.

Matt ended the call and decided to explore his surroundings while he was alone. It was less curiosity and more of an attempt to keep his mind from settling until he could ask Maggie some *real* questions. Ones that she did have answers for. Like the investigation into Erin's accident.

He imagined his late wife as he often did. Years later and he could still trace every curve of her face in his mind. Bright eyes, button nose, all smiles. He felt more at home in those snatches of memories than he ever had since the accident. Matt didn't know if that was because he'd moved on or that he hadn't.

Depending on the day he could give an answer one way or the other.

Today, though?

He wasn't sure.

The inside of Maggie's house was surprisingly cozy, all things considered. Beige and white, linens, blue and yellow pops of color and various pictures of Cody, herself and a few people Matt didn't recognize. He didn't know what he had expected of the ex-reporter—maybe newspapers and magazines scattered around or a bulletin board filled with pictures all connected by strings—but normal hadn't been it.

He moved from the living room to what he guessed was a converted dining room currently being used as an office. At least this room looked more like the speed of the Maggie he remembered. Surrounding her computer was a sea of notebooks, papers and empty coffee mugs. A small filing cabinet was tucked next to the desk, partially hidden by a wooden side table standing over it. Matt walked closer to inspect it. There was a lock on the bottom drawer.

A treadmill was tucked in the corner and against the left wall, while a small bookcase stood on the right and seemed to be dedicated to Cody. Colorful spines filled the openings while toys were interspersed between some of the covers. Matt paused at one and smiled. It was a toy cop car.

From there his attention roamed over the pictures hanging on the wall in this room. A collage of more unfamiliar faces hung above the desk while a picture of a newborn Cody sat in the center. He'd had a lot of hair as a baby and was swaddled in a blue blanket, filling up the entire image.

And then there Erin was. Heralding a memory of the first time they'd talked about having kids. He'd just joined the Riker County Sheriff's Department and she was working through nursing school. They'd decided to wait until their life became less hectic.

Now here he was, years later, standing in Maggie Carson's house wondering what his own child might look like.

It was another question he didn't have an answer to. However, it shepherded in a thought that had been in the back of his mind as he moved around the house, looking at pictures.

"Investigating and snooping are separated by the finest of lines, Detective Walker. I thought you of all people would know when you're toeing it."

Maggie came to a stop at Matt's side. A sweet aroma wafted off her, filling his senses before he'd known what hit him. Shampoo or soap or perfume. He didn't know which but it didn't matter. It caught him off guard all the same.

"Don't worry, I know the urge to not answer a question is hard to resist," she continued. "Did you finally get some insight into me? Find anything interesting, Mr. Keen Eye?"

She was teasing him. There was a small smile pulling up the corners of her lips. It caught his attention and held it for a few beats too long. It also applied pressure to the idea that he despised the woman next to him. That she was nothing more than a pain in the ass. *His* ass.

Maggie put a fist on her hip. She must not have liked his slow response time.

"Oh, come on, Detective," she said more harshly. "Make an observation about me based on what you've seen. Wow me with your skills."

"It's not as loud as I thought it would be," he started, rising to the challenge. "The house I mean. With how you present yourself in public *and* one-on-one I assumed this place would be...more chaotic. Instead, it's pretty calm. Ordered. Except in here."

He motioned to the desk and the scattered papers around her computer.

"But I bet my badge that all of those are just for show. I can't imagine someone like you would leave any important documents out like that. Even in your own house. I imagine those are tucked inside that filing cabinet." Matt motioned to the coffee cups next. "I also assume you work at home, considering the amount of coffee cups on your desk and the treadmill. I bet you use it when you get tired of sitting around all day. Unless I'm wrong and you work late nights instead." He walked over to the toy cop car. "And if I had to take a stab in the dark about *this*, I would bet you tried to talk Cody out of this toy, explaining that cops are too by the book for your liking."

Maggie's eyebrow stayed high. She raised her hands in mock defense.

"Your words, not mine," she said. "But anyone could have drawn the same conclusions if they'd just walked through the house. Especially if they already knew me or, at least, *of* me. It's not a hard stretch to see a treadmill and coffee cups in an office and guess the person works at home."

There was no smugness there but Matt did recognize a challenge when he heard one. Maggie was baiting him to prove himself.

So he did.

Dropping any hint of a smile from his lips he walked back over to her desk. He pointed to the baby picture of Cody. Her smile wavered before he even spoke.

"You adopted Cody," he said simply. "The house is filled with pictures of him as a toddler but this is the only one I've seen of him as a baby. And it's cropped, which means you weren't the one holding him."

Like a candle that had been lit, Matt could almost see her intention to tease him start to burn away. She crossed her arms over her chest.

"I suppose if you make enough guesses you're bound to get one right." Her smile had dwindled down to barely there but he wasn't reading anger from her. "The first time I met Cody he was three." She motioned to the picture of him as a baby. "That was the only picture that had been taken of him until he was placed in foster care. I make sure he knows that even though I wasn't there, I still like to look at how cute my baby boy was."

"He knows he's adopted, then."

Maggie nodded.

"There's nothing wrong with being adopted," she said, resolute. "And I wanted to make sure he knew that at an early age. I'm sure he'll have more questions when he's older but so far, he's never had any problems calling me Mom. Even if I tell him it's a little too formal sounding. But he's a mini genius so I guess that comes with the territory."

This time the smile grew. Love. Pure and genuine.

Matt might not have known Maggie Carson as well as he'd once thought but in that moment he knew one thing for certain. She loved her son with all of her heart.

He opened his mouth to say something when his ringtone went off. The caller ID read "Ryan Ansler."

"That was fast," Matt muttered. He looked at Maggie before pressing Accept. "Give me a minute."

THE DRIED BLOOD had washed away easily enough in the shower but that didn't mean Maggie wanted to push her luck by blow-drying her hair. The gash left by the bat wasn't bad enough to need stitches but it was still throbbing enough to be uncomfortable. She stood across from her reflection in her en suite, trying to see if the past two days were showing.

She felt tired and her legs were a little sore. The former could have been attributed to the sleep she'd gotten off and on in the hospital but the latter was troubling. Matt had been right about her working from home and using the treadmill when she felt too cooped up or restless. She wasn't ready to knock out any marathons but over the past few years she'd gotten into fairly decent shape.

So why were her legs sore?

Had she walked around a lot the day before?

Had she run?

Maggie raked a hand through her hair and blew out a sigh. She'd always loved puzzles. Mysteries had to be solved. Questions had to be answered. That was all she'd ever wanted to do when she was little. Find the truth that people—bad people—tried to hide.

But now that the new mystery involved her?

She hadn't asked to lose a day's worth of memory. And well, she didn't like the feeling.

Just as Matt hadn't asked to lose his wife. Or have Maggie start her own investigation during what must have been the worst low of his life like some dog after a bone.

Again she sighed.

"You in here?"

Maggie straightened as the detective called into her room. One last look at her reflection and she nodded.

"Yeah," she answered, walking out to meet him in the hall. His eyes were wide. Something had happened. "Was that the sheriff?"

"No, Detective Ansler. But we do have some new information."

Again, Maggie searched his expression. It was

troubled. The cold knot that had formed in her stomach earlier started to expand.

"And I'm guessing it's not the answers to all of our questions."

Matt shook his head.

"CSU reported in," he started. "Your prints and Dwayne's were found on the bat. A partial print was found on the inside of the screen door near the handle. And that's it."

Maggie felt her eyebrow rise.

"What do you mean *that's it*?"

"I mean those are the *only* prints in the entire house."

Her eyes widened.

"And that's not normal."

Matt shook his head. Again, he didn't like what he was saying.

"No, that's not normal for a lived-in residence," he replied. "Unless Dwayne has a serious case of OCD, that house should have been covered in his prints at the very least. Which means one of three possibilities."

Maggie held up her index finger, much like the sheriff had done earlier in the hospital.

"One, that Dwayne wiped down the entire place after he was beaten into unconsciousness." Maggie held up another finger. "Two, *I* wiped the place down before I did my own unconscious dance."

Matt held up his finger in lieu of her ticking off her third.

"Three, whoever attacked both of you wiped the place down, erasing any evidence linking him or her to the house. And to you and Dwayne."

That cold in the pit of Maggie's stomach was starting to unravel to the point of becoming flat. She had no sarcasm or joke to replace it. There was no denying she was caught in the middle of something.

And she needed to figure out what that something was fast.

Maggie gave the detective one decisive nod. He must have seen the intent in her eyes. Ever so slightly he tilted his head to the side. The human way to silently question something that was a mystery.

Under different circumstances, she would have liked to have been a mystery that the handsome Detective Matt Walker tried to solve, but now she was afraid the question mark she had been branded with was dangerous.

"Okay, then we only have one option." She brushed past the man and headed for the living room. He followed her, his stare burrowing a hole in every step she took. He kept quiet as she grabbed her purse and dumped its contents on the floor next to the couch. "Let's figure out what I did yesterday."

His eyes didn't leave hers for a moment. Then he nodded.

"I agree. I also want to call in CSU to dust for prints here. They're still working on the partial, but considering how quickly you appear to have left yesterday, maybe if you did have company, we can at least find out who it was."

"Good idea."

Maggie was still trying to ignore how freaked out it made her feel to know someone or something had spooked her enough to run from her own home. Her eyes started to skirt over the various pieces of her life that had made up the inside of her purse when she realized Matt wasn't moving.

Maggie looked up and met his eyes.

Trying to solve another mystery.

But not one that had to do with her.

"After I make this call you're going to answer a few questions before we do anything else." His voice was cold. She could almost swear she felt its chill from where she sat on the floor. He wasn't going to let her off the hook this time. She'd run out of wiggle room.

"Sounds fair."

Matt pulled out his phone but kept his eyes on her when he spoke again.

"And we'll start with why you think my wife was murdered."

Chapter Six

Erin Walker had been walking out of a three-story parking garage when the truck popped the curb and hit her. She was a tall woman and her height was the only reason she went over the top of the truck instead of under it. Though that stroke of luck wasn't enough to save her. She was gone before she hit the ground.

Maggie had been working for the *Kipsy City Chronicle* at the time. She'd been gunning for the news editor position that was about to open up when she heard the accident over the police scanner. Wanting to get the scoop before another reporter who'd shown interest in the promotion did, Maggie had grabbed a notepad and pen and drove like a bat out of hell to get to the parking garage. The drive hadn't been a long one. She arrived before any patrol officers, just after the EMTs.

That was when she saw Erin for the first time. From a distance she looked like she was sleeping. Like she'd decided, instead of going wherever it was she had started to go, that she'd lie down on the side of the street, wrapped up in her long blue coat and ready to fall asleep beneath the stars. Then the rest of the details had begun to filter in. Erin hadn't been the only hapless victim. An older man who'd had the misfortune of being on the side of the road next to the opening of the parking garage had also been struck. He, however, was surrounded by EMTs. His name was Lowry Williams. He survived for two days before he succumbed to his injuries. According to everything she discovered, he was a good man.

And also the reason Maggie didn't let go of what happened.

"Lowry Williams passed away before he was able to talk to anyone other than the emergency responders and hospital staff," Maggie started. She really didn't need to remind Matt about that. The detective might not have believed her back then or even now, but he'd done his due diligence and learned every angle of what had happened. Or so he thought. "Except that he did talk to someone. Me. Lowry didn't have any family so I pretended to be a friend. I'm not proud of the lies I had to tell to convince a nurse to let me see him but it worked. He let me slip in to see him before he was wheeled out to surgery. It was the last time Lowry was conscious. Afterward the nurse realized I was a reporter and, to cover his hide, told me to leave. I imagine he never mentioned me to anyone else to, again, save his hide."

Matt's expression was blank.

"And what did Lowry say?" he asked, voice void of any notable emotion.

"He was in a lot of pain," she reminded him. "He spoke in broken thoughts and I can't even be sure my questions were understood by him. But there was something he said twice that stuck with me after I asked what happened. 'She waved at him.'"

Matt's body shifted. He dropped his hands to the top of his belt.

"She waved at him," he repeated. "Who waved?"

"He was in so much pain but I assumed he meant Erin." Maggie wanted to look away from the detective, to give him privacy with his thoughts at the mention of his late wife, but she had to press on. She had to make her point now that he was willing to listen to her. Even if it was only because it might be dangerous not to know. "It was such an odd statement that I couldn't let it go. I went back to the parking garage and tried to track down the security footage from either the parking garage camera or the one across the street. But the parking garage tape had already been taken by the police and the one across the street had a ticket in for repairs." Maggie cut her gaze downward for an instant. The detective might not like her next admission. "So I decided to take a closer look into Ken Morrison to try to find a connection." Matt's body tensed enough that Maggie knew just saying the name of the driver who had killed Erin was dangerous. Even if Ken was no longer living.

"Since they spent that night trying to stabilize him

after his overdose, getting into the hospital to talk to him was a no-go," she continued. "And then, after he passed, I spent some time tracking down relatives and friends, trying to find a connection between him and Erin. Trying to figure out why she would wave to him."

"I'd never met him or heard of him before the accident," Matt interrupted. "Erin's coworkers and friends also had no idea who he was until that night."

"But I kept looking anyway," she admitted. "I just… I started looking into Erin instead."

Matt's face drew in, his lips pursed and his eyes turned to slits.

"You started looking into Erin?"

Maggie knew now was not the time to back down from what she'd done. From the decisions she'd made. From the detective. So she rallied herself, shoulders going stiff and back straightening.

"I started with her coworkers first and then friends. I looked at her online profiles. I was just trying to find a connection to Ken outside of the accident. One that would explain why she recognized him and waved to him before everything happened."

"And did you find one?" Matt forced out each word. "After you decided to pry into my wife's life for some damn story, did you at least find a connection?"

Maggie tried to hide the sting she felt at his accusation but she didn't correct him. It wasn't important now why she'd done the things she did then. Her intentions changed nothing. She shook her head.

"No, I couldn't find a connection. For all I knew he could have waved to her and she did it in response. But it didn't matter because although that's what grabbed my attention, it was what I found next that held it." Maggie grabbed her keys off the coffee table and got up to lead the detective back to her office. She unlocked the bottom drawer of her filing cabinet and began to rustle through it with one file in mind.

However, it wasn't there.

"What the heck?" she muttered, going through the files again. Matt moved around to her side and peered into the drawer. "I had it here," she explained. "A folder containing everything about what happened. But it's not here."

"It was a folder?" Matt asked. Maggie nodded. She turned her attention to the detective when he swore beneath his breath. "And did it have a name on it? The folder?"

Maggie didn't like the look he was giving her but she nodded.

"I always intended to take the information to you when I had something. Something *concrete*. It has your name on it."

Matt pulled out his phone. He swiped through a few pictures until he found the one he wanted. Maggie inhaled as he turned it around for her to see.

The picture was of her, unconscious and on the floor. A bat was in one hand and a folder was next to the other. She didn't have to use the zoom function to read the red print across the top of it. She knew what it said.

"That's the folder I'm looking for," she said. "Do you know where it is now?"

"In evidence." Maggie started to sigh in relief. Matt ruined it. "But by the time I got to Dwayne's house the folder was empty."

Maggie froze.

She might not have her memories of what had happened but she knew one thing for sure.

"I decided a long time ago that the only reason I'd take that folder out of this house was to bring it to you." Her hands fisted at her sides. "But now I don't know what I figured out!" Anger was starting to burn through the outside edges of her chest, coming closer to the heart of her. Where it was born from, she couldn't tell. But she didn't like it. Maggie turned her full gaze on the detective. "Do you know what the truth is, Detective?"

Matt raised his eyebrow.

"The truth is I gave up on this case within the first year of the accident," she continued without waiting for him to respond. "I was tired of being the only one who thought there was another layer to it. That there was some kind of conspiracy going on. That Ken Morrison wasn't just some drug abuser who destroyed the lives of three people, including himself. I was tired of everyone hating me for believing there was more." Maggie threw her hands wide, motioning to the house around her. "So when I hit too many dead ends, I stopped looking. I stopped asking questions. I got a new job. I started a family. I tried to redeem my image from, as you've said and as I've done, an ambulance chaser. I even joined a book club. *I stopped looking.*"

Maggie felt her anger turning to something else. A raw emotion she hadn't realized was waiting to be unleashed. She took a step to the side and glanced at the filing cabinet.

"Something must have happened yesterday that was big," she said. "I wouldn't have brought this all up again if I wasn't sure I'd found something."

Fear.

That was what she felt. Beneath the surface of sarcasm and sass, fear was lurking. Sure, throughout the past four years she'd thought about Erin's and Lowry's deaths but she'd kept those thoughts private. After she'd confronted Matt about her suspicions back when it had happened, she'd created a county of enemies. It had made her reevaluate her life. Her drives, her goals, even her career. But to bring the case back to the front lines? That was dangerous, not only to her emotions but also to the life she'd spent the past few years building. To a life she had fallen in love with. To a son she would cross oceans for.

She turned her gaze back to the detective. He searched her face. She hated how vulnerable she felt at that moment. How could she complain about what she'd lost when he'd lost the woman he loved?

"What *did* you find back then?" he asked after a

moment. "What was in the folder before yesterday?" His voice was like velvet. Smooth and strong and fluid. He took a step closer. It helped pull Maggie out of her widening hole of anger and fear.

She took a deep breath and answered, "A list of names."

"Names? What names?" he started. "And where did you get the list from?"

Maggie wished she'd had her files now. It would have made her explanation easier. Still she straightened her back again and got ready to try to convince the detective that the list was not only important, but might have been the key to that night years ago, too.

However, Maggie didn't get the chance.

The world around them filled with a nearly deafening sound. Maggie instinctively tried to escape it by ducking her head and covering her ears. The detective wasn't far behind, throwing his body around hers. Maggie gasped into his chest as another burst of sound sliced through the air.

This time Maggie could place it.

It was glass. Shattering glass.

Someone was breaking the living room windows.

MATT'S HAND WAS on his gun as soon as the noise stopped.

"Get away from the windows," he barked, already pushing Maggie back. He didn't want her out in the open if the next one was broken.

He unholstered his gun and moved into the living

room, senses on high alert. Both windows were broken and glass was scattered on the floor. In the middle of the shards next to the window that looked out to the street sat a brick, highlighted because of how out of place it looked against the light carpet.

Matt's gaze snagged on movement outside the front window. Right through to a van at the curb. And getting into that van was a man wearing a baseball cap.

"Hey, you!" Matt yelled. "Stop right there!"

Matt flung open the front door just as the van's door slammed shut. The tires squealed as the van began to peel away.

It presented Matt with a choice.

He could leave Maggie and chase the man who may or may not have been behind the attack on her and Dwayne or he could stay with her and call in the fleeing culprit. The first ran the risk to himself and to Maggie. The second ran the risk of letting their only lead get away.

Matt holstered his gun and hesitated.

And then Maggie ran up behind him and grabbed his hand.

"Come on," she yelled, moving out the door and trying to tug him along. "We'll lose him if we don't hurry!"

"We can't go!" Matt yelled. "It's too dangerous!"

But Maggie wasn't having it. She paused only long enough to look him square in the eye and say one sentence with absolute conviction.

"Matt, my son could have been in there!"

That was all it took to push his good sense to the side.

Maggie must have seen the change in his expression; she continued to pull him to his car.

This time he let her.

Matt had the pedal to the floor as soon as they were in, trying to eat up the gap between them and the van, but the closer they got the more erratic the driver became.

"Call this in to the Darby Police," Matt said as their mystery perpetrator took a turn out of the neighborhood so fast he popped the curb. The driver overcorrected and clipped the neighborhood welcome sign at the corner. It splintered but didn't break apart. The van kept going like it hadn't hit it at all. "This guy's driving is going to get himself killed."

"Just make sure it's not us who get killed," Maggie replied. Even in his periphery he could see her leaning forward, tensed, while her hand clung to the handle above the passenger-side door. He was feeling it, too. Danger and adrenaline. Both mixing together to feel like an odd form of excitement. That feeling was starting to pull out an unintended reaction in him. The corner of his lips quirked up.

"With my driving skills? I don't think so." He eased them out of the neighborhood without losing much speed. The van was hauling down a two-lane that stretched straight for a few miles before getting into the thick of Darby. No cars were on the road, which probably was normal for this time of day during the week, but that didn't mean they were in any less danger.

"Was that Detective Walker being cocky?" Maggie asked with a nervous laugh as Matt tried to gain back some speed. He hated to admit the sound bolstered him.

"That was Detective Walker being confident in his abilities," he responded. "But still we need to call this in." He fished out his phone and tossed it to her. "Call 911 and put it on speaker so we can tell—"

Matt cut himself off as the van slammed on its brakes. He followed suit, lurching both him and Maggie forward. The space he had just been trying to close between the two vehicles disappeared so rapidly that by the time the Jimmy came to a stop they were within throwing distance.

"What's he doing?" Maggie asked, all traces of excitement replaced by caution. In the next second the man answered. His reverse lights blinked on. "He's going to hit us!"

The van lurched backward so fast that by the time Matt put the Jimmy in the same gear, the driver had already changed his course again. He cut his wheel so the van turned, giving Matt a clear view of the driver's-side window. It was rolled down. Which gave the man pointing a gun at them an uninhibited view.

"Get down!"

Matt threw his arm out to make sure Maggie stayed down just as the windshield shattered over them. Another shot sounded. The Jimmy sank to the left. Before Matt could bring out his own gun to the party, the sound of screeching tires squealed away.

"Stay down," Matt barked. He pulled his gun out and up, ready to return fire but the van was already booking it in the opposite direction, dust kicking up behind it.

"They're fleeing," he said with a few added words that would have made his mother angry. "Are you okay?"

Maggie popped up like a spring flower.

"We have to follow him," she yelled. "We can't let him get away!"

Matt knew now that the right thing would have been not to bring Maggie along. Just the option of staying at the house after someone had thrown a brick through the windows until backup arrived would have been risky before. Now the option of following had proven to be far too dangerous. To keep following would be nothing less than reckless. But he wasn't about to spell that out for her. Not when she wanted blood.

Instead, he reached over and grabbed his phone. She started to argue again that they needed to continue the pursuit but he ignored her until the local police dispatcher picked up the phone. Even if Matt agreed with her and decided to risk her life further, the fact of the matter was whoever it was they had been chasing wasn't just some petty criminal fleeing a crime scene.

Matt looked out the window at his front tire. Their perp had shot it flat.

Whoever the man was he had a lot of guts. And determination.

Matt glanced back at his deflated tire.

The man knew what he was doing.

Which made him even more dangerous.

Chapter Seven

An off-duty Riker County Sheriff's Department deputy was the first to arrive at the scene. He parked his car on the shoulder behind where Matt had moved the Jimmy off the road.

"You're fast," Matt greeted the man. His name was Caleb Foster, and while he'd had a rocky start when he'd first transferred in, he had earned the respect of the department. And a lot of their friendships, too. Matt hadn't had the chance to really get to know him but he knew that would change soon. Especially since Billy had suggested the man try for a future detective's spot opening thanks to a growing county.

Caleb raised his eyebrow.

"If the sheriff called you roaring like he was, you'd get to where he told you to as fast as you could."

"You're right about that," Matt agreed. He'd called Billy after he'd gotten off the phone with the Darby PD. To say the sheriff had retained his calm and cool composure after finding out someone had shot at one of his people would have been a bald-faced lie. No

one attacked one of his own. Not without incurring
his wrath.

"I wasn't too far away, though. Just dropped the
dog off at the vet for a checkup." Caleb walked closer
and lowered his voice. He motioned to Maggie, who
was on the other side of the car, facing the trees
that lined the road. She had his phone up to her ear.
"How's she doing?"

"Have you ever met her before?"

"No. Can't say I have."

Matt let out a long breath.

"I don't think I've met a more stubborn woman in
all of my life," he said. "I'm sure she's only rattled
when she wants to be."

He glanced over as Maggie turned, her face in
view. She'd been cut by the windshield's glass in two
different places. When he'd first asked about them
she'd shooed away the concern. Seeing her hurt,
though, even if the cuts were small, filled him with
more anger than he thought was possible.

"But I'm not above admitting I don't like this situation," Matt added. "We need to figure out what the
hell is going on. Fast."

Caleb agreed and together they recapped what they
knew until the Darby PD showed up. Two officers
relayed the infuriating information that the van and
the driver hadn't been found. There was an all-points
bulletin out, and officers were looking but so far all
they had was a big bag of nothing.

They needed another lead. Another angle that

might shed light on what was going on. A wish they got when Caleb drove them back to Maggie's house while another deputy stayed with the Jimmy when it was being towed.

Caleb whistled low, pulled out his gun and followed Matt around. Together they cleared the house for the second time that day and waved Maggie in. She hadn't said much since they'd been stranded but after the high of being in a pursuit had worn off she had asked to call Cody's school to make sure he was okay, just in case.

Now her lips were downturned, her eyebrows drawn together and an emotion he couldn't pin was brewing behind her eyes. Her hands were on her hips as she walked through the front door and turned toward her living room and its floor littered with glass shards. The defensive stance only strengthened an impulse within Matt he had been trying to ignore.

He wasn't angry at Maggie Carson. He was angry *for* Maggie Carson. A change that he would have laughed at had anyone suggested it was possible the day before.

"Didn't you call in a CSU crew already? Before the bricks came flying in?" Caleb asked, actively trying not to touch anything while still looking around. Matt had explained their theory about Maggie leaving the house the day before in a rush. He didn't combat it with a different one after seeing her car keys on the table.

"Yeah, Sheriff Reed said he was going to person-

ally call them when we got off the phone earlier."
Matt shared a look with the deputy. They both knew
that meant that the crew would be there sooner rather
than later. "So until then we have to be careful with
what we touch," he added on for Maggie's benefit.

She was standing next to one of the bricks, leaning
over to get a better look at something. The movement
caused her hair to fall over her shoulder. It created a
backdrop of curls that somehow made her profile even
more appealing. He shook his head a little, hoping the
deputy hadn't caught the lingering look. Since when
did he focus on Maggie Carson like that? Especially
in the middle of an active crime scene?

"What if there's a piece of paper on the other side
of the brick?" Maggie's eyes stayed aimed downward.
"And what if we aren't patient people and want to see
what that paper says right now?"

That definitely caught Matt's attention.

"There's paper under the brick?"

Maggie nodded.

"I'm assuming the message is meant for me, seeing as there's a rubber band around it and the brick.
Not to mention it crashed through *my* window into
my house."

True to her word there was a piece of paper bound
to the brick. Matt turned to Caleb.

"Do you happen to have any rubber gloves in your
car?"

The deputy shook his head.

"I'm driving my girlfriend's car while mine is in the shop."

"I'm almost afraid to ask if you have any," Matt said to Maggie. She raised her eyebrow but then cut off whatever she was about to say by holding her index finger up.

"Would a plastic sandwich bag work? They're pretty useful, you know."

Matt smirked but was weirdly proud of the suggestion. He nodded and a minute later he was navigating the rubber band off the brick and holding up a letter, sandwich bag on his hand.

The note was written on stock printer paper and torn in a few spots but the message across its middle was clear enough. At least the first part. Understanding it was a different story.

CHRIS LESLIE RYAN was written in small, neat black print. An equally small line in red ran through the name.

But Matt still didn't understand.

"Who is Chris Leslie Ryan?" he asked the room, though really it was rhetorical in nature. He didn't expect Maggie to react. Not as much as she did, at least.

In another moment of open vulnerability, her hand went up to cover her mouth and her eyes went wide. They met his gaze with a surge of nearly tangible fear. For that one second every part of Matt felt drawn to those green eyes, felt compelled to replace the fear with anything else.

"Who is Chris Leslie Ryan?"

Maggie shook her head and lowered her hand. As if she couldn't believe the answer she had.

"It's not one person," she said. "It's three."

MAGGIE FELT HERSELF shutting down, freaking out and attempting to keep her chin up all at the same time after she escaped to her bathroom. The thick skin she had cultivated when being a cutthroat journalist had been her greatest goal in life, and had apparently grown paper-thin over the past few years. Or she'd finally come up against something that was sharp enough to cut through it.

She looked at her reflection in the bathroom mirror for the second time that day and tried to grab some piece of solid ground from the day before.

Nothing but a headache and sore legs.

The sound of strangers in her house clobbered through the sanctuary-like feeling her bedroom and en suite used to hold. She finished patting water off her face and paused next to her bed. Before she had a chance to explain the note, a CSU crew had arrived. Even without being a part of Matt and the deputy's inner circle she knew that the sheriff must have been the devil that was nipping at the crew's heels. They were already apologizing for the delay before they'd even hit the front porch.

It was all good timing, though. As soon as she'd seen the names Maggie knew she needed a moment to collect herself. Seeing how the detective's expression had changed after *she* had read the note had proven that she hadn't been wearing her game face. And that was what she needed if she was going to survive this situation.

She needed to stay strong.

She needed to stay steady.

She definitely didn't need to lose her mind. Again.

Heavy footsteps echoed down the hallway. Maggie pulled a smile out of her arsenal, hoping it would provide cover for her actual feelings. Detective Walker came into view.

"You look grumpy," she couldn't help but say.

Matt didn't even skip a beat.

"Why do you think Chris Leslie Ryan is actually three people?"

He stopped just inside the doorway and crossed his arms over his chest. Maggie wondered when the last time he slept was. He looked like a man who was ready to fall face-first into a bed.

The bed next to her suddenly felt like it was on fire.

Maggie angled her body slightly so she couldn't see it.

"Because I don't know a Chris Leslie Ryan," she answered. "But I do know a Chris, a Leslie and a Ryan."

The detective shrugged.

"Those are pretty common names," he pointed out. "I also know a person who goes by each."

He was trying to make Maggie create a solid case for herself. It was an effective way of getting answers without asking any questions. She understood the tactic. But that didn't mean she liked feeling as if she was blowing something out of proportion. Not again. Not by Matt Walker.

Like her mother before her, to make her point more *pointed*, Maggie's hands gravitated to her hips. She even felt her chin tip up. All business.

"Well, unless you were married to a Chris, adopted a child from a Leslie and currently work for a Ryan, then maybe my Chris, Leslie and Ryan are a little more relevant than yours. Don't you think? Not to mention, once again, the brick went through *my* window."

The detective's expression gave away only one clue as to his first thought. Surprise. But at which point, she didn't know. Then, like watching a clock, she saw the gears starting to turn. His eyebrow rose and he stood straight.

"When's the last time you saw Chris?"

Maggie hoped she hid the involuntary twinge of pain at how casual the question sounded. Chris Bradley wasn't the happiest of memories for her.

"When we signed the divorce papers," she said, trying to maintain an even voice. "Four years ago. Give or take."

He glazed over the admission to his next question. "And Leslie?"

"She helped navigate the ins and outs of adoption but she relocated shortly after the adoption was finalized. The last time I saw her was maybe two years ago?" Maggie held up her hand to stop the question before he asked it. "Ryan is the owner of the magazine I work for. I mostly work out of my home but stop by the office at least once or twice every month. I saw him last week."

"So there's no connection between these three people?"

Maggie shrugged.

"The only connection I know is that they've been part of important life moments for me," she admitted, a knot beginning to form in her stomach again. "If there's something else that ties them or us together, I don't know it." Maggie's air of calm ran out. She took a step forward and lowered her voice so the team in the living room couldn't hear her. Not that she distrusted them.

Maggie realized the movement might simply mean she *trusted* Matt.

Maybe.

"Everything that's happened in the past two days," she started. "Surely it's not all a coincidence? There has to be *something* connecting everything together that we're not seeing. Right?"

The detective didn't answer right away. He was still searching for something. The answer? Or the right way to say the answer?

"Maggie." His voice was deep. Smooth. The only sound in her world at that moment. "I think it's you. I think you're the center of it all and that message might have just proven it."

"How?"

She needed the truth. She needed it so badly that she moved closer to the man. On reflex she tilted her head back to better meet his stare. Had they ever been this close before? And was it her imagination or did he look down at her lips?

"The message," he repeated, derailing her unwelcome thoughts. "It proves that whoever wrote it either *knows* you or researched you well enough to get really personal information."

"But why? Why would I need a reminder if I know him already?"

Maggie already didn't like what he was going to say. A storm seemed to start up in his eyes. Deep eyes, drenched in mystery.

"My guess? He's saying that he doesn't just know you. He knows your past and your present." She watched as the detective's jaw hardened. He was angry. "It's a threat, Maggie. A personal one."

Chapter Eight

His plans changed as soon as he said his theory out loud. Again. Right in that moment, standing so close to Maggie Carson that he could smell her shampoo. Someone was sending her a message and, while he didn't know exactly what it meant, he wasn't going to stand for it.

He was going to protect Maggie and her son to the ends of the earth if he had to. No discussions. No hesitation. No second thoughts.

"Pack a bag for you and Cody," he commanded, hoping the authority in it would keep her from arguing with him the way only Maggie could argue with him. Still, he added on an explanation to move things along. "If someone thinks he knows you and your life, then we're going to do some things you don't normally do."

Maggie's eyebrow quirked up so quickly that he realized what he'd said sounded charged with something other than protectiveness. He took a step back to create some distance between them, playing it off like he was getting ready to go into the living room.

"And that would be?" she asked, looking down at his feet for a second as he moved away.

"We're going to get you out of here for one. You two aren't staying the night here." He motioned toward the front of the house when her mouth opened to interject. "Unless you want Cody to stay here. In the house that the gun-wielding, brick-throwing perpetrator has already targeted and perhaps even been inside."

"Of course I don't want him to stay here," she snapped. "I just—I don't have anyplace for us to go." Like a match had been struck, Maggie's cheeks turned red at the statement. The sight surprised him. He felt his expression soften. If only for a moment.

"Don't worry," he said. "We'll figure it."

There was no snappy reply; Maggie simply nodded.

Half an hour or so later and Billy didn't have good news. Matt shouldn't have been surprised. Not with how everything else had been going.

"They found the van you chased behind a Walmart in Kipsy. It had been set on fire. By the time first responders arrived the car was covered." Billy's jaw was tight. The three of them stood in the kitchen, just out of earshot of two CSU team members who were finishing up. "There was no security footage around that got a good shot of where it happened but there was definitely no body in the vehicle."

"So the gunman who charmed his way into my house via bricks isn't some first-time criminal, I'd guess," Maggie piped in at his side. "He knew how to cover his tracks."

Billy tipped his head to the side in agreement.

"I wouldn't count his intelligence out," he concurred. "But I also wouldn't say he's making all smart decisions. Instigating an attack in broad daylight against a law enforcement officer isn't the best course of action."

"He probably didn't know that he was a detective," Maggie said, jutting her thumb over to Matt.

"Which means that, while he might be familiar with you, Ms. Carson, he's not familiar with Detective Walker here."

"He at least didn't know my personal vehicle," Matt agreed.

"Which makes me feel inclined to agree with your plan." Billy lowered his voice again. "We'll set you and Cody up in a hotel in Carpenter, a few minutes' drive from the department, and put a guard on you."

Matt saw the slight shift in Maggie's demeanor. She was uncomfortable. And Billy didn't seem to catch it. His expression didn't change as he spoke directly to her.

"Do I know this guard?" she asked, eyes sticking to Billy's.

Was that what was making her uncomfortable? Who the guard would be?

Billy motioned to the front yard.

"Deputy Caleb Foster has offered. When you head over to the hotel he'll meet you there." Billy glanced at Matt. "Once you all are there Detective Walker *will* go home and get some rest."

That was an order, given in a no-arguments tone by the sheriff. It kept Matt quiet. This time Maggie looked at him. She didn't say anything, either.

"Until then, we need to get a better handle on this situation," Billy continued. He dug into his pockets and pulled out his keys. He tossed them to Matt. "Take the Bronco and see if you can retrace any of her steps before Cody gets out of school."

"Shouldn't we get him now?" Maggie jumped in. "If our mystery person knows me then he definitely knows where my son goes to school."

"Which is why Cody has his own guard. Do you know my chief deputy?"

"Suzanne Simmons," Maggie said with a nod. "She had an impressive résumé even before her promotion when you took over as sheriff."

Billy smirked.

"That's her. Impressive to the teeth. Great at her job. Cutthroat when needed." He sobered. "She's also the godmother to my kid. Not to mention she's a mother, too. She won't let anything happen to Cody."

Maggie visibly relaxed a fraction.

"Detective Ansler is still working this case," Billy continued. "You keep him in the loop. And, Matt, you call in at any sign of trouble. You *do not* take off after it. Am I understood?" Matt nodded. "Good. I don't need to send the Bronco to the body shop again. I'm still in the doghouse for slamming it into a house last year."

"Hey, I appreciated that."

They turned as Deputy Foster walked over. Billy was referring to when he'd intervened in a wild rescue of Caleb and his now girlfriend. Both men shared a quick smile.

"All right, let's go pick up your dog and then head back to the station," Billy said, conversation over. Caleb pulled out a card from his back pocket and handed it to Maggie.

"Call me if you need anything before we go to the hotel."

Maggie took it and gave a small smile.

"Okay."

Matt didn't know how it happened but there it was. Jealousy. Just sitting there in the pit of his stomach, unhappy at the idea of passing Maggie off to someone else.

Someone who wasn't him.

Get it together, Matt scolded himself.

But still that feeling stuck even as Caleb and Billy walked off.

"Wait!" All three men turned to Maggie. She was looking at Billy. "I know enough about the sheriff's department and the people who work there to know that you consider them more than just colleagues. And you and Matt are friends. Good friends." She hesitated. It was a strange reaction to see in her. Even stranger was the look she gave Matt before continuing. "He doesn't like me. A lot of law enforcement around here doesn't. So why are you doing all of this? Most people would have kept me in cuffs in the first place and now I'm going to ride in your personal vehicle while the godmother to your child watches mine? I get that you're the sheriff but that seems a little bit beyond the call of duty. Why help me, of all people, like that?"

Another feeling Matt didn't like replaced jealousy. He didn't have time to address it before Billy answered.

"You already said it. I'm the sheriff and you're a resident of Riker County who needs help." Billy flashed a genuine smile. "There's nothing that I won't do to help my people. It's that simple."

MAGGIE WAS GRATEFUL for the sheriff's candor. She wasn't special in his eyes, which was somehow comforting. It was like she had a clean slate again. Like she hadn't fallen in the eyes of Riker County law enforcement yet. Now she was just a resident of the county who needed some protection.

And answers.

However, those were trickier to get as proven by the stoic set of Matt's shoulders as he walked from the spot on her front porch to the Bronco she was sitting shotgun in. He left behind a man from CSU who disappeared back into her house to finish whatever it was that he was supposed to be finishing.

"What did he say?" Maggie greeted. Matt answered by swearing.

"Let me guess, they didn't find anything. Again."

"They found the prints they believe to be ours from today," he said, voice constricted with frustration. "But like Dwayne's house they are almost positive your place was cleaned. Where there should be prints of you and Cody there are none. Which doesn't help us."

Maggie's stomach turned.

"I'm now one hundred percent for staying at a hotel with a guard," she decided. "This is getting too creepy."

"We can go there now, you know," he replied matter-of-factly. "To be honest it would be much safer for you than running around the county grasping at straws until school lets out. Detective Ansler and I will keep looking for leads no matter what."

It didn't sound like a dismissal but Maggie still felt the sting as if he was trying to get rid of her. She bristled at the thought.

"Listen, I might not be a cop but I did *something* yesterday that created chaos for everyone. Whether we like it or not that everyone *includes* you and myself. That means we have a better shot at figuring this thing out. Together. So even though you'd rather be detecting with someone else, it's me you're stuck with for now. Okay?"

To her surprise Matt chuckled.

"You sure are bossy for someone who technically is still a suspect."

"By *bossy* I'm sure you mean *determined*," she replied, pushing her shoulders back. Her attention went down to the purse in her lap. She'd started to go through its contents when the man had stopped them from leaving the house to update Matt. CSU had allowed her to take the bag and the contents she'd poured out onto the floor. Now she was sifting through the items in hopes of finding a clue.

"So is there anywhere you think we should go?" Matt asked. She could feel him watching her. "Anything in there jumping out at you? Anything bringing back some memories?"

Maggie cycled through scraps of paper and cards that had been in her purse for upward of two years.

"I'm remembering all of the times I promised myself I would clean this thing out." She set the stack of scraps on her thigh and picked up a new handful of odds and ends. "Yesterday apparently wasn't the day I decided to follow through."

The detective laughed again. This time it was softer.

"Erin once lost her engagement ring in her purse. She forgot to take it off before work and had to drop it in there."

Maggie kept her gaze down. She didn't want to spook the man from opening up. No matter how much it shocked her. Whenever they had talked about Erin in the past it had been one-sided with her trying to get him to agree with her theories on Erin's death. And that at that time, Maggie was positive his beloved had been killed on purpose. Targeted by Ken Morrison. Not just a random victim. Maggie was more than happy to hear nice stories rather than speculation of the reason behind the young woman's death.

"How long did it take her to find it?"

"Two days. I kid you not. We turned that thing inside out and still managed to miss it until we thought it was long gone. Then *bam* she reaches into her purse for some gum and comes out with the ring. I couldn't believe it had been there all along, but she said the Bermuda Triangle is at the bottom of every woman's purse. How things disappeared and reappeared there was a mystery."

Maggie didn't have to see his smile to hear it.

"Well, she wasn't wrong." Maggie was smiling, too. Though she knew her patience was about to turn tail and run. They needed a lead. Not to bond.

Matt kept the car in Park as she continued to sift through the remnants of her life that had never made it back out of her bag. Old receipts, notes for work, a few fast food napkins, a pack of tissues, five pens, allergy medicine, two canisters of lipstick and four plastic dinosaurs that Cody had insisted they take with them to the park one day last month. Nothing out of the ordinary...

"Wait."

Maggie pulled out a card she almost mistook for more paper scraps and notes. Her handwriting on the back didn't help.

"'Two-hundred-one,'" she said, reading the card before flipping it over. "This is new."

Her eyes traced the words but no sparks of recognition flared.

"Looks like we're going to a hotel after all," she continued. "Just not the one the sheriff had in mind."

She handed him the card.

"Country Heart Hotel," he read. "In Kipsy. What's there?"

Maggie shrugged.

"Hopefully answers."

He turned over the ignition and started their drive away from her home. It bothered Maggie more than she thought it would. It wasn't like she was leaving the house forever. Then again, someone didn't like whatever it was that she'd found out. What if the next time the unknown man came back he issued more than just a threat tied to a brick?

Thankfully she didn't have to dwell on that thought for too long. The detective handed his phone over and told her to call the hotel.

"We need to see if that room is occupied. If so, then we're calling for backup," he explained. So she sweetened her voice, called the room and, when no one answered, called the front desk and asked if the guest had already checked out.

"He did," the man at the front desk confirmed. "Would you like to book it?"

Maggie politely declined at the detective's insistence.

"He said *he*," Matt pointed out.

"So do you think I met the mystery man there yesterday?" Maggie was relieved in part that she hadn't been the one to book the room. "And what? Now he's trying to threaten me?"

Matt shrugged.

"Maybe you tried to get the information to someone else after I wouldn't bite."

But who would that have been? Maggie wondered as silence stretched between them for a few miles. Matt finally broke it.

"The list of names you found," he started. "We got interrupted before you could tell me who they were and where you got them."

Maggie felt around inside her purse again until she found a pen. She took an old sticky note with her grocery list on one side and flipped it over. Taking in a deep breath, she jotted out three names, then she let that breath out slowly.

"I might not have the original list but I won't forget their names," she explained when he gave her a questioning look. She traced her handwriting before continuing, "I researched them for almost a year straight. And I asked *you* about them, too, but it probably wasn't the best time to do it. I doubt you remember them."

Matt's hands gripped the steering wheel for a moment. Then they relaxed.

"After the funeral." It wasn't a question. How could either forget that afternoon? Regret filled Maggie's chest.

"I'm sorry," she answered instead. "I should have approached you somewhere—*anywhere*—else. I—I just felt like I was running out of time. I was desperate. But still I shouldn't have—"

Matt held one hand up to stop her. Maggie quieted.

"We can't change the past," he said, voice thrumming into a low octave. Not a sensual tone but a decisive one. "But we might be able to right some of its wrongs. Now, tell me about the names and where you got them. And maybe we can solve this damned mystery and let everything get back to normal."

Maggie wanted the same thing but couldn't deny she once again felt a surprising sting. Their normal was two different paths. Without any intersecting points.

Completely separate from each other.

That had never bothered her before. But now, for some reason she had trouble understanding, it did.

Chapter Nine

"Joseph Randall. Jeremy Pickens. Nathan Smith."

Maggie waited to see if the detective recognized any of the names. He shook his head. "There's quite a few of each in the United States as you can imagine. And definitely more than a few in Alabama."

"Feels a lot like grasping at straws."

"And that's how I felt until I found news stories on all three names." That got the detective's attention. He kept his eyes on the road but she could tell he was focused on her. "Without going into all the research I had to do and all the phone calls, emails and lies I had to tell to get the information, here's the basics. Joseph Randall, early thirties, died in a head-on collision in Florida almost a decade ago. Jeremy Pickens, also in his thirties, died in a fire started by faulty wiring at his home in Georgia eight years ago. Nathan Smith, forty, was hospitalized after a mugging turned more violent. He succumbed to injuries in the first few hours of being admitted to the hospital. That was six years ago in Tennessee."

Matt didn't say anything right away. It gave Maggie a moment to look at him in profile. Strong jaw. Prominent nose. Stern lips. Those same lips were downturned. He hadn't known about the list and he didn't know about the men on it. She wished she could hear his thoughts. Instead, she'd have to settle for another one of his questions.

"And where did you find this list?"

Maggie sighed.

"You're not going to like this answer," she warned. A muscle in his jaw jumped.

"Maggie."

"It was taped to the top of Erin's locker at work. Which is probably why you didn't see it when you cleaned it out."

Matt went tense again. She couldn't blame him.

"And the hospital just let you back into the nurses' locker room?"

Maggie looked at her hands.

"I might have done some sneaking around."

Matt said some not-so-great words. She waited for more but was surprised when it was himself that he cursed.

"*I* should have found the list."

Maggie started to reach out for the man, to try to comfort him, but caught herself. They could talk about all the things they should and shouldn't have done later. Right now they needed to focus.

"I contacted a friend up north in law enforcement and, as far as he could tell, there was still no connection between the names on that list and Erin. Or Ken, for that matter. Why she had those names and where she got them from, I never learned." She blew a breath out. "And to be honest, that's when I started hitting all of the road blocks. A wave and a list of names taped to the top of a locker does not a conspiracy make."

"But now that list is missing and there's a very real person threatening you to be quiet," he added.

She nodded.

"There is that."

They lapsed into another silence. This time it wasn't that bad. Maggie chalked up the detective's quiet to him silently processing the new information. Most likely trying to track back memories of his wife to figure out why she had the names in the first place. Or maybe his lack of sleep was starting to get to him. He wasn't sitting as tall as he had been on the ride over from the hospital. Either way, Maggie watched out the window as the small town of Darby was replaced by the much larger city of Kipsy and tried to give him privacy. She felt the weight of weariness starting to press on her bones, too. Even though it was barely afternoon, it felt like days had passed between the hospital and walking through the back door of her house. An ache had begun to beat in her chest as she thought about Cody at school, oblivious to everything bad that had happened. Maggie prayed they could find the answers they needed before the three-o'clock bell rang.

It wasn't until they pulled up to a two-story building that didn't look like it had more than two stars, let alone five, that Matt broke the silence with a low whistle. He pulled into a Country Heart Hotel parking spot next to the front doors and cut the engine. Worry started to fill Maggie's gut.

"Are you sure this might have something to do with your investigation?" Matt asked. "And not something...well, else? You know, something *personal*?"

Maggie turned on the man like he'd thrown a bucket of ice water on her. She felt heat scorch up from her belly, across her neck and into her face.

"And what exactly are you trying to suggest, Detective Walker?"

Matt held his hands up in defense.

"Nothing illegal or anything like that," he answered. He jabbed his finger out the window. "I just meant this place kind of looks like the type where a person might meet a special kind of person when they wanted some alone time. I didn't know if you had someone like that in your life right now."

"And you thought that if I did, that yesterday, the day I potentially made some big discovery in an investigation that destroyed my reputation, that I decided to visit some imaginary—what?—*lover* here instead of at my house or his?"

"Hey, you said you can't remember anything from yesterday."

"Still, I'm pretty sure I didn't have a rendezvous with a secret lover," Maggie said. "Considering I'd need a secret lover to do that." The detective lowered his hands and for a split second Maggie thought she saw relief in his expression. It made the heat in her cheeks reach a new height. "And if that was your way of trying to see if I have a boyfriend, next time just *ask*."

The detective's lips thinned. For a moment Maggie wondered if she'd crossed some imaginary line between them. It was pretty foolish for her to think, even for a second, that Matt Walker was relieved she was single.

What was also foolish was to admit she liked the idea that *he* might be relieved.

What am I, in high school? she thought.

Wanting anything beyond their forced proximity acquaintanceship wasn't just barking up the wrong tree, it was barking up the wrong tree in the wrong park. Plus, she'd only spent less than *one day* with the man. Why was she entertaining *any* thoughts about him like that?

Those storm-fueled eyes found their way to hers.

They were grounding, an anchor that kept her still.

Oh, yeah, she thought. *That's why.*

"The one fact that we have to work with is that you don't remember what you did yesterday," he said. "I'm trying to cover all of our bases. Even the personal ones. Remember that, other than Cody telling us you made him breakfast and took him to school, no one can account for you yesterday. I'm just double-checking there isn't someone who *could* and you haven't brought it to our attention."

Maggie's dichotomous emotions of anger and, dare she think it, latent desire started to dissolve. Maybe she was reading too much into one look. Matt *was* just doing his job. She took a small breath.

"No, the list I gave you in the hospital contained the only people who I might have talked to or seen on a normal day. Even abnormal, if I'm being honest." Maggie handed Matt the hotel manager's business card that she'd found in her purse. "I think I came here because someone asked me to. There's no other reason I would be here or take a card with me and write down a room number. I've never been here before. I wouldn't have picked this as a meeting place unless someone else picked it."

Matt held her gaze for a bit longer. He must have believed her. He nodded.

"Then I want you to stay here while I go talk to the manager and staff." Maggie opened her mouth but Matt hurried on. "We have no idea what went down here yesterday. Your presence might distract them. Plus, I can't imagine you'd stay quiet long enough for me to even ask the right questions."

"That's insulting," she tried, knowing it really wasn't. Because that was exactly what she would do.

Matt pulled out his phone, clicked a few buttons and held it up in front of her.

"That's the truth and we both know it. So I'm

going to take a picture of you and show it around instead."

Maggie narrowed her eyes at the phone.

"Now, smile for the camera, please. We don't want to scare them. We just want to question them."

Maggie changed her frown into what she hoped was a smirk to end all smirks. A *click* sounded as the picture was taken.

"How'd I do?" she asked, half sarcastic, half curious.

The detective snorted.

"You look like a pain in my side." He cut her a quick grin. "And I wouldn't have expected it any other way."

TECHNICALLY, MATT WAS off duty but the hotel manager named Luca, a small man who appeared to be in his fifties, didn't know that. He looked up as Matt walked in and his eyes immediately went to the badge around his neck. Matt rarely wore his credentials like that but he'd found that when the badge was hanging in view that most people remained pleasant during questioning. Luca, however, looked at the badge once before his eyes glued to Matt's face. He was already fidgeting by the time Matt walked up to the front desk.

"Hey there. I'm Detective Matt Walker from the Riker County Sheriff's Department and I'd like to ask you a few questions, if that's all right," he greeted, cutting out any pleasantries.

Luca nodded his head so hard that Matt was afraid it would come right off.

"Yes, sir, whatever you need!"

The way he spoke was an immediate red flag. He was nervous. *Really* nervous. Matt had gone from asking some simple questions to mentally preparing for the fact that he might have to unholster his gun. Something wasn't right. And he was about to find out if it had to do with a brunette ex-reporter currently confined to the sheriff's car.

"Were you working yesterday?" Matt started off.

Luca nodded. "I run the hotel during the weekdays."

"And did anything out of the ordinary happen here yesterday?" Matt followed up. "With any of your guests? Or staff?"

"Out of the ordinary? I don't—I don't think so. Can you give me an example?"

Luca's eyes widened but he seemed not to have expected the question. Which was good news for Maggie. She apparently hadn't done anything that was outrageous during her time there. At least, not publicly. Matt pulled out his phone and the picture he'd just taken of Maggie.

"Have you ever seen this woman before?"

Luca squinted his eyes. He nodded a few seconds later.

"Yeah. She was in here yesterday."

"She checked in?"

"No, she bought a sandwich."

He pointed to the corner of the lobby. A counter

containing a coffee maker and foam cups stood next to a vending machine and a small display refrigerator. Prewrapped sandwiches, cups of fruit and bottles of orange juice and water lined the three shelves. It was more than Matt had expected to see in the place.

"She bought a sandwich," he deadpanned. "And that was it?"

"She asked if she could have a Ziploc bag," Luca tacked on. "She said she wanted to save one half for later because she wasn't that hungry."

Matt kept from rolling his eyes. It was hard.

"No, I mean, did she check in or out or talk to anyone else while she was in here?"

Luca didn't have to think about it long at all.

"When she paid she said she was meeting one of the guests."

"Did she give a name?"

"No, and I didn't ask for one. To be frank, usually when a pretty woman like that meets someone here during the workweek there's a spouse, or two, out there who have no idea. I try to keep out of it." Luca's eyes widened. That nervousness that had greeted Matt came back in full force. "Is that your wife?"

Matt had done his fair share of interviews during his career with the sheriff's department. He'd been called names, insulted, questioned and even physically attacked. In each instance he'd kept his cool and responded without issue. However, the hotel manager's simple question had an unforeseen effect on him.

Was Maggie his wife?

In an instant two threads of thought wove together. One was of the wife he'd had for two years. The one he'd met in a grocery store in Carpenter. The one who laughed at all of his lame jokes, loved pineapple on her pizza and would fight anyone who disagreed, and who promised to love him always in front of a church full of people. The one who had called to remind him to do the laundry because she needed a fresh pair of scrubs for work the next day. The one who, an hour after that call, was gone.

The other thread, the one that caught him wholly off guard, was of a woman who had entered his life at its lowest. A woman who had ambushed him time and time again during that lowest part, trying to convince him that what he knew was a lie. A woman whom he'd denounced in front of a county's worth of people and publicly hoped he'd never see again. A woman who, years later, was still not giving up. A woman who had grabbed his hand and pulled him out into the world to chase a suspect, despite the obvious danger. A woman who had driven him crazy but now was surprising him more than he thought was possible.

Was Maggie Carson his wife?

No. But she was turning out to be much more than an ex-reporter running after a story.

In fact, Matt was starting to see that maybe he'd misjudged her all along.

MAGGIE WAS BORED. Or, rather, impatient. While the detective did his detecting inside the lobby, she kept her word by staying put in the car. From her seat she'd taken in everything in her view from the rocks lining the flower beds to the flagpole that needed a good deal of repair. She'd even watched as a giggling couple dressed in workday best made out next to their cars before getting into them and driving off in separate directions. After that Maggie realized her listening to Matt Walker's commands wouldn't last.

She opened the door, got out and quietly shut it back. Instead of going into the lobby, she decided to pass through the breezeway that led to the courtyard that all room doors faced. Since it was a weekday and barely afternoon to boot, there was no one lounging in the pool or on the slightly rusted-out patio furniture around it. She turned around in the courtyard and read the second-floor room numbers until she saw 201.

"I hope there's something in there that will make sense," she mumbled to herself, rounding the deep end of the pool to head for the stairs beneath an awning.

However, two steps along the pool's side, something caught her attention in the water. Thinking it might be trash, or maybe just her imagination, she paused and bent over the edge to get a better view.

The pool probably wasn't the most used part of the hotel but it was still kept up enough that the water wasn't cloudy. Something *was* at the bottom of the pool, resting near the drain in the middle of the deep end. Whatever it was it looked to be the size of her palm, maybe a little bigger, but the depth and water warped the image. She couldn't tell what it was but it didn't look like trash.

It looked like something in a bag.

A jolt of adrenaline made Maggie stand tall.

"No way," she said to herself, glancing up at room 201 and then back at the breezeway that led to the lobby. She would have had to cross right by the pool to get to the room and to leave it. Her heartbeat sped up as she looked back down at the object in the pool, but she already knew she'd made up her mind.

Now she needed to be fast.

Chapter Ten

Luca conveniently couldn't find the guest book. He also had a hard time remembering who the man who'd checked into 201 was. The only details he could cobble together were that he walked in the morning before six, paid in cash and left his key at the front desk while Luca was in the bathroom around ten. When Matt pressed for anything else, the hotel manager began to sweat. The man nearly seemed to have a heart attack when Matt asked if he could see the security footage for the hotel.

"Do—do you have a warrant?" he asked. "Because I—I don't think you can unless you have a warrant."

That was when Matt figured out why he was so nervous at law enforcement being in the hotel.

"Listen, I'm going to level with you, Luca," he started, leaning on the counter, trying to appear casual. "I've been on the job long enough to know what kind of establishment you're running here. On the outside this hotel looks normal, a little run-down but still good for a night or two. A good place, as you said, for cheating spouses to meet secret lovers. I get that. I do. But considering how nervous you seem to be, I'm pretty sure you play to the rougher crowds rather than to unhappy men and women in business suits. Maybe drug dealers or buyers? Sex that's paid for? You might even be in on the action. Either way I'm sure all your loyal customers pay in cash while you conveniently lose the guest book a lot. Am I right?"

Matt's hunch was confirmed. Luca's face went beet red. He opened his mouth like a fish out of water but Matt didn't have the time to listen to lies.

"If today were any other day I wouldn't be standing here, asking for your cooperation. I'd be telling you," Matt continued. "But today's timeline is a little tight. Instead of calling in my friends at the local office, who maybe even know you already, I'm going to leave. Only after I get to look at the security tapes for yesterday. I'm looking for one man and one man only. You can keep your tapes afterward. So what do you think? Are you going to help me out or is this place about to be swarming with black-and-whites?"

Matt wasn't planning on calling in anyone if Luca refused to let him see the security footage. He couldn't just waltz in and demand them without a warrant. But if you said something with enough confidence then sometimes that did the trick.

And it sure did it on the hotel manager.

"I—uh—I'll get them," he said after a moment. "It might take a minute."

Matt pushed off the counter and smiled.

"Good. While you do that I'd like to go ask your staff about the occupants of 201." Matt paused and dropped his smile. "If that's okay with you?"

The question seemed to ease the man a little. It gave him the illusion of control. It made him stand taller as he nodded.

"Yes, sir."

He saw him out and told him that housekeeping might still be in the laundry room preparing the new towels before they made their rounds. The handyman wouldn't be in for another hour.

Matt took off his badge and placed it in his back pocket. If there were any guests with an aversion to cops he didn't want to find out by being ambushed. He'd rather blend in. Maggie, on the other hand? He almost laughed at the idea of telling her to try to keep a low profile.

And then he cursed under his breath.

Maggie wasn't in the Bronco and he didn't know why that surprised him at all. He sighed, turned on his heel and headed through the breezeway. Knowing her, she was either already asking the staff questions or trying to break into room 201.

Matt scanned the courtyard, ready to be annoyed when he found her, but was distracted by something that turned his blood cold. There was something in the pool. *Someone* in the pool.

He waited a beat to see if the person was moving,

stilling every instinct he had to dive in, when he saw it. A cloud of brown hair.

Maggie.

Every part of his body seemed to react at once, leaving only thoughts of the woman behind. He tore off his holster and phone and was in the pool in what felt like a second flat. Diving into the deep end, Matt opened his eyes beneath the water.

And indeed confirmed it was Maggie.

However, she definitely wasn't in distress. In fact, she wasn't even in her clothes.

Oh, hell, he thought just as her eyelids lifted. Two forest green eyes found his moments before she pushed off the bottom of the pool. Her body flew upward past his face. He followed her. He could already hear her yelling at him before he even broke the surface.

"What do you think you're doing?" she yelled, wiping water out of her eyes. "You scared the heck out of me!"

"Me?" he responded just as loud. "What are *you* doing? And why aren't you wearing any clothes?"

"I didn't want them to get wet," she countered. Like he was looking at some picture book, trying to find Waldo, he spotted her pants, blouse and shoes on the other side of the pool. "And I *do* have clothes on! I'm not crazy!"

Matt didn't know which part of her statement he wanted to dissect to try to make sense of the maddening woman treading water in front of him in nothing but her underwear.

"Then what are you doing in the damned pool?"

She raised her hand out of the water only to point down. On reflex he followed the silent order but his gaze got caught on a black lace bra he'd definitely not planned on seeing that day. It pushed up a fair amount of cleavage; even beneath the water it was distracting.

"There's something at the bottom of the pool I was trying to grab before you scared me half to death," she answered, unaware that his gaze and thoughts had strayed for a moment. "What are *you* doing in the pool in *all* of your clothes?"

Matt strung together a series of curses, his frustration at the woman almost a tangible object.

"I was trying to save you," he defended. "I thought you were drowning. One second you're in the car and the next I see you floating in the pool. Forgive me for jumping to an illogical conclusion."

Where he was sure Maggie would kick up a fuss or, at the very least, goad him, she instead seemed to lose her initial anger. Her expression softened. Somehow it had seemed to ease his anger, too. He looked back down at the object she'd pointed to, this time avoiding looking at her body.

"It's a clue," she said, answering his unasked question. "I think I threw it in here yesterday on purpose. To hide it. Or keep it safe."

Matt didn't need another word. He held his breath

and went under. This time his descent didn't have his heart slamming against his rib cage. Instead, he scooped up the bag at the bottom of the pool and pushed while relief settled through him.

Maggie was okay.

Maddening, but okay.

"Well?" she asked as soon as he sucked in air. "What is it?"

A door shut somewhere behind them. Matt whirled around, trying to shield Maggie's body from view. A young man paused, eyes widening at the sight of them, before going to Matt's gun on the side of the pool.

"Take this," Matt muttered, pushing the bag back to her under the water. He misjudged where she was and his knuckles touched bare skin. She didn't make a fuss, though, and took the bag.

It freed up Matt's hand to pull his badge from his back pocket.

"Police business," he said loud enough to break the young man's gaze from his gun.

The man hesitated. Matt didn't break eye contact.

"Move along," he commanded. Even to his ears Matt heard the hammer drop in his tone. The young man didn't say anything but hurried past them and out of the breezeway.

"We need to get out of this damned thing," Matt muttered. "Come on."

Maggie didn't argue and together they waded to the shallow end of the pool. It wasn't until Matt was standing on the patio, picking up his gun and cell phone, that he remembered that he had been the only one fully dressed. He glanced back across the pool and froze.

He'd seen half-dressed women before. Lacy bras, sexy panties, bare stomachs, legs and more. But looking on as Maggie stood next to her clothes and stared down at the bag in her hands, Matt felt like he was seeing something new. Or, really, feeling it. Her face was angled downward, her wet hair dark against her sun-kissed skin. The little makeup she'd put on that morning had washed down her cheeks. Her brows began to knit together just as her frown deepened. Still, he couldn't ignore one truth about the woman any longer.

Matt might have thought a few bad things about Maggie throughout the years but he realized he'd never once thought she was anything other than beautiful.

Even when she was being a pain in his ass.

"Maggie, put on your clothes," he chided, breaking out of his epiphany. He rounded the pool, already annoyed at how his clothes clung to him.

Maggie didn't move. At least not toward putting on her clothes. She held the bag up to him instead.

"It's a key," she said.

"What does it open?"

For the first time that day Maggie looked tired. She shrugged.

"I have no idea."

THE SECURITY FOOTAGE was grainy and only covered the main entrance of the lobby, not the lobby itself.

"That's convenient, considering there's a side entrance," Maggie muttered.

Matt leaned his head to the side.

"Convenience is this hotel's biggest selling point." Normally that was the point of a hotel but judging by his tone, Matt didn't seem to be a fan of the establishment.

The mystery man who booked room 201 wasn't seen by the lone working camera. However, Maggie was. She pulled into the front parking lot around ten in the morning in her personal car and left fifteen minutes later.

Maggie didn't like what she saw in the footage, but kept quiet until they were back in the car. Alone.

"I was scared, Matt. In the security footage I looked scared."

Matt started the engine.

"I know."

Maggie looked at the hotel one more time as they pulled away, trying to grasp the memories she'd lost by sight alone. Instead, she decided she didn't like the place at all. She wasn't alone in that opinion, either. Matt had had a private chat with the hotel manager while Maggie dripped water in the middle of the lobby and it had been clear neither enjoyed it. She wouldn't be surprised if Kipsy PD made a stop by the hotel sooner rather than later.

"So we have to talk about that bag in the pool."

Matt was going in the opposite direction of Darby, which probably meant Carpenter, and the hotel was their destination. At this point Maggie didn't mind. She had her packed bag with her and was ready to rinse off the chlorine and change. Considering the detective was still dripping a little, she imagined he, at the very least, needed a good towel. "How did you know it was you who left it? Did you remember doing it?"

Maggie readjusted in her seat to sit taller. She was quite proud of herself in this instance.

"When I transitioned into working for the magazine, I toyed with the idea of trying my hand at starting a book, true crime. A nonfiction book about cases in Riker County—because you have to admit we've had some doozies around here." Matt inclined his head. He couldn't argue with that. No residents could. "Anyway, I ended up spending basically two years with my head in other true crime stories and learned a lot of interesting things. Including how this man almost got away with murder by wrapping a piece of evidence in a plastic bag and dumping it in the pool. Two days later, when he was alone, he came back for it and tried to dispose of it. He was caught and eventually went to jail. I in no way condone him or what he did *but* the idea of what he did never really left my mind. I've actually always wanted to try it, just to see if it really does work, but we don't have a pool and it's not like I'm about to go to the community one with a sandwich bag, rocks and a mystery item to test it.

Today I noticed the rocks outside the hotel and so I figured I did yesterday, too. I don't know where I got the bag from, though. Unless I brought it with me."

Matt held up his index finger.

"I think I can help with that."

He told her about the sandwich she'd purchased with the cash she'd had on her, according to the hotel manager. Plus the Ziploc bag.

"Ten bucks you only wanted the plastic bag," he continued. "You must have sneaked around, grabbed some rocks and tossed it in. None of the hotel staff said they saw anything."

Maggie looked down at the bag in her lap. A handful of small rocks and one small silver key.

"But why did I hide it? I arrived at the hotel alone and I left alone. Why not just take it with me and hide it somewhere that wasn't in a public place?" Maggie ran her hand through her hair. Wet tangles fell against her shirt.

She glanced at the man next to her as he laughed.

"Listen, if there's one thing I've learned in the past—" he made a show of looking at his thankfully waterproof watch "—four hours or so is that Yesterday You is a mystery wrapped within a mystery and crammed into another mystery. I think we're better off working with what we have instead of trying to retrace your steps."

Maggie sighed.

"Not that we have much of a choice." She shook the bag. "This is the only concrete lead we have now… And it's a small key that leads to where? I don't know."

"Could it fit your filing cabinet?" Matt offered, coming to a stop at a light. They were definitely headed toward Carpenter. In front of them was the county road that transitioned from downtown to the rural edge of the neighboring town. "Didn't the drawer that originally had the file in it have a lock?"

Maggie shook her head.

"The key to that is gold *and* on my key ring. I never went to great lengths to hide it because I never thought anyone would ever look for it." Matt reached over and took the bag from her. He lifted it up to look at it more closely.

"It could go to an actual lock. Is there anywhere you might have one?"

Maggie shook her head again. She hated not having better answers.

"Unless I bought one yesterday, no."

They sat in silence as the light turned green. Maggie was trying to list the ways she would use a lock that fit the key.

"What if this isn't mine?" she asked. It was more to herself than the detective. "What if I got this from our mystery man somehow? I'm almost scared to think what it might be used—"

Maggie didn't have time to scream.

Something slammed into the driver's side of the Bronco.

And then the world flipped.

Chapter Eleven

The world was dark. At least Matt's world was.

It also was painful. His entire left side ached, including his head. It was throbbing.

But why?

He opened his eyes slowly and didn't understand right away. Instead, he blinked at broken glass and metal. He was lying on his side. Glass and metal beneath him there, too.

What had happened?

Noise began to filter in as his head swam, lost in a sea of confusion.

Someone was screaming.

"Matt! No!" It was a woman. *"Matt!"*

The fog of confusion lifted in an instant and he knew what had happened. Someone had hit them, they'd flipped and now the Bronco was lying on its side, the driver's-side doors pinned against the ground.

And the woman screaming was Maggie.

Matt turned his head so fast the pain tripled. He fought the urge to get sick. Though the empty passenger's seat hanging above him wasn't helping. The door was also missing.

"Matt!" Maggie shrieked in the distance. She sounded terrified.

What was going on?

Matt tore the seat belt off him—probably the only reason he was still alive—and scrambled to pull himself up to stand. Pain surged across him. Not only was his left side hurting but so were his ribs. He sucked in a breath, grabbing his side on reflex. His hand brushed against the butt of his gun. Thank God for holsters.

"Help! Matt!"

Maggie's yells were pitching higher.

Matt readied to answer when a new voice entered the mix.

"Shut up or I'll go back and kill him," a man yelled. It seemed like their mystery man had found them.

Again.

Matt grabbed the passenger seat, pain no longer something he cared about, and pulled himself up through the truck. The fact that he was having to use the Bronco as a jungle gym meant that they had indeed flipped after the initial hit. And the fact that the passenger's-side door was completely gone meant that it had been violent. No wonder he'd lost consciousness.

He hoped Maggie hadn't been seriously hurt.

Matt unholstered his gun and used the seat as a foothold to push himself out of the vehicle. The

Bronco was in the middle of the intersection. No other cars were around but one. It was a truck and Maggie was being pulled toward it.

Matt threw his legs over the side of the Bronco and jumped to the ground. The noise caught the man's attention. He whirled around, pulling Maggie against his chest like a shield. Matt's gun was up and aiming within a heartbeat.

Immediately he noticed two things that weren't great.

The man had his own gun and it was pressed against a wincing Maggie's stomach. She looked at Matt with fear clear in her eyes and blood across her face. A new cut had stretched above her right brow and was bleeding at a good clip. It had to have been stinging her eye.

The second detail that kept Matt's stomach tight was the fact that he could see the man's face clearly. He wasn't wearing a mask. Nothing to obstruct their view. Which was never good for a hostage. And that was exactly what Maggie would be if Matt didn't stop him.

"You move any closer and I'll shoot her," the man yelled. "I mean it!"

Matt didn't lower his weapon. But he also didn't move from where he'd stopped at the front of the Bronco.

"If you shoot her, I'll shoot you," Matt replied. "Simple as that. So let her go."

Matt clocked the man's age as midforties. He was

tall but broad; Matt guessed he would be able to do some damage if he had to go one-on-one. His hair was thick and black, his skin tan, and he was dressed not unlike Matt was. He looked like an everyday man. One whose hand was steady.

He wasn't nervous.

Which made him even more dangerous.

"I'm not going to do that." His voice carried over the few yards between them with ease. Like he was a man used to talking to people. Maybe even giving them orders. There was no awkwardness in the way he addressed Matt. Perhaps he'd even done this sort of thing before.

"And I'm not going to let you take her," Matt promised. The man wasn't the only one with a steady hand.

"Then we have a problem."

He pressed his gun harder into Maggie's stomach. She winced. Matt reacted on instinct and took a step forward. The man pulled Maggie a step backward.

"What do you want?" Matt tightened his stance, already contemplating if he could get a clear shot without harming Maggie. "Who are you?"

"It doesn't matter who I am, but what I want is *simple*." The man pulled the gun up to the side of Maggie's head. Her eyes locked with Matt's.

"To be left alone," he bit out. "Once and for all."

Matt shook his hand.

"Listen here, buddy. You're the one who's been following us. You threw the first stone. Brick, if you want to get technical. You can't blame us for trying to find you."

The man snorted. Matt was too far away to hear it but he saw the expression of disbelief clearly enough.

"Considering this one here hasn't let me go in five years, I'm afraid I can't shoulder the blame of starting things first."

Matt's blood went cold.

"Five years?" he asked. Maggie's eyes widened. "What do you mean by that?"

The man's face went blank. Like an invisible hand had taken an eraser to the emotion that had just been there and scrubbed it clean. He didn't answer and for a few seconds the only noise in the intersection was the sound of two broken vehicles whining. It wouldn't be long before some motorist came along. They were in a slow part of town for the time of day but not that slow.

"Let her go," Matt repeated. He didn't like the change in the stranger. If he was becoming unbalanced then that only lessened Matt's chances at getting Maggie back unharmed. "Let her go and we can talk."

Maggie opened her mouth to say something but Matt gave her a look that kept her quiet. The man's eyes narrowed.

"I know her." The hand gripping Maggie's arm must have tightened. She winced again. "She won't let *this* go." For the first time the man's gaze shifted away from Matt. He looked down at Maggie, his expression still blank, but she only had eyes for Matt.

They widened and then trailed to the side, away from the man and to the ground. Before he could question it she did it again. Eyes on him and then jumping to her side. All within the space of a few seconds. By the time she started to do it again, Matt realized what she was trying to tell him.

"Maggie," he warned. But he should have known better. When their mystery man's attention went back to Matt, the infuriating woman went into action.

She stomped down on his instep with a small war cry. The man matched it as he howled in pain. It was enough of a distraction to take advantage of. Maggie threw all of her weight to the side she'd been looking toward. She broke free of the man's grip.

Then everything seemed to happen in slow motion.

The man recovered enough to know he needed to do one of two things. Shoot or run. Fight or flight.

Matt had to make the same choice in less time. To fight was to put Maggie, who was out in the open, in danger. To flee was to leave her in danger. Two roads but the same scenery.

If Maggie was at risk either way, then Matt was going to choose the former.

He needed to stop the man once and for all.

Matt stepped forward and pulled the trigger.

The man didn't have time to retaliate. Instead, he tapped into his flight reflexes and moved. Still, the bullet found his arm. He yelled out in pain but kept his head. As he turned to run he shot back blindly.

"Matt!" Maggie yelled out.

Pain burned across his thigh as a bullet must have grazed him. He didn't have time to check. He dived to avoid another shot and fired back. The man, however, was faster than Matt would have thought. He made it to the cover of the truck.

"Maggie, run!" Matt yelled, moving full tilt toward the vehicle. There wasn't much else in the way of cover unless he wanted to fall back to the Bronco. And he didn't want to create distance; he wanted to close it.

Out of his periphery Maggie did as she was told but not without making a little noise.

"He took the key, Matt," she yelled back as she ran. "He took the key!"

Matt almost stuttered in his movements. Not only had this man repeatedly put Maggie in danger, but he also potentially held the literal key that could help explain Maggie's theory about Erin's death.

He made it to the truck without another shot being fired. Matt didn't have to be a mechanic to know that the vehicle was a lost cause. The man wouldn't be able to drive it anywhere, let alone use it to escape this situation.

"Come out with your hands up!" he yelled.

The sound of a car door slamming behind him drew Matt's attention. An elderly man was standing beside his car, stopped at the intersection next to the Bronco.

"Get back in the car!" Maggie yelled, changing direction to go right to him.

Another noise brought Matt's attention back to the truck. Footsteps. *Retreating* footsteps.

Fed up with hide-and-seek, Matt rounded the front of the truck with his gun raised just in time to see the man running over the sidewalk and to one of the buildings by the intersection. It was two stories and run-down, abandoned, he'd guessed, since no one had come outside at the sound of the crash or the gunshots. Or maybe they were playing it smart and were staying put. Hopefully calling the cops while they were at it.

"Stop," Matt yelled. "Stop or I'll shoot!"

The man sidestepped around the front of the building until he disappeared along its side. He didn't shoot but that didn't mean that Matt wouldn't. If he got another clean shot, he'd try to take the man down. To temporarily disable him so he couldn't run anymore. This needed to end. For Maggie. For Erin. For the truth.

Matt paused at the corner of the building and looked around the edge, keeping his head low. The man wasn't anywhere to be seen. Matt cursed beneath his breath as he tried to catch up.

His adrenaline was on high, surging through every muscle in his body. When a door at the back corner of the building flung open, he nearly shot the teen who walked out.

"I—I heard a—" He started to stutter, stopping so quickly that he nearly toppled over. He was looking at the gun as if it was the first time he'd ever seen one in person. And maybe it was. Either way, Matt hoped it would be the last. At least for the day.

"I'm a cop. Get back inside," Matt barked, lowering the gun. "Lock this door!"

The boy didn't have to be told twice. He scurried back into the building in a flash. Matt kept his gun low just in case more civilians were about to spring out at him. He'd never accidentally shot a civilian and didn't want this to be his first time.

The building led to an alley that opened back out into the street. Matt paused, heart slamming against his chest. The man could have easily gone around the next building or out to the road. He didn't want to lose him. He couldn't.

A scream cut through the air, making the choice for him.

"Maggie!" he yelled, running full tilt down the alley. How had he already gotten to her so fast? Matt didn't think his lead had been that large.

He skidded to a stop the moment he hit the sidewalk along the road.

It wasn't Maggie who screamed.

"Stop or I'll shoot!" the man yelled, opening a repeat of their earlier conversation. However, this time the scene had changed. The man was standing next to a running car, the driver's-side door open and the driver standing at the end of his gun. He must have made her stop and pulled her out.

Matt had to admit, it was a good move as far as escaping was concerned. Especially considering the woman he had at gunpoint was pregnant. Young, too. Her eyes were saucers as she looked at Matt.

"Whoa, whoa," he said. "Easy there."

The man's calm was gone. He didn't seem shaken, but angry was definitely on the table.

"We're not doing this again," he growled. "You drop your gun and let me leave or I'll show you what I'm capable of."

"Let her go so we can talk," Matt tried.

The man moved the gun from the expectant mother's side to her protruding belly. She had to be at least eight months.

Matt needed to tread carefully.

"You don't know this about me so I'll go ahead and tell you," the man started. "But I don't kill women. However, I'm not above hurting them." He pushed the gun into the woman's belly. She whimpered. "Now, I won't say it again. Drop the gun. Or I'll give you something to regret for the rest of your life."

Matt didn't try to get any more information. He wouldn't take the chance. Slowly, he dropped the gun on the ground and then nudged it away with his foot. He placed his hands in the air.

The man also didn't waste time. He pushed the woman away from him. She turned tail and ran toward the intersection in the distance. Then the gun was pointed squarely at Matt. He was at the mercy of the stranger.

"Were you responsible for the death of my wife?"

Matt hadn't realized how much he believed Maggie's theory until the moment he asked the question. He'd tried to stay objective, following potential leads that connected Maggie to what had happened to Dwayne. But somewhere in the past few hours, he'd gotten in line with her idea that Erin's death was no accident. That it had been a part of a larger picture. That Ken Morrison hadn't just popped that curb because of some ill-fated destiny.

The man kept his gun steady. His words matched.

"If I were you, Detective, I'd find another case." He lowered himself into the car but kept the door open to give Matt one last message. "*I* don't kill women. Don't make me start."

Chapter Twelve

The pain in Maggie's leg was nauseating. Not to mention there was a growing list of other aches radiating throughout her body. Her hand was already covered in blood after swiping at the stream coming down into her eye from the cut across her forehead. It stung something awful, but that didn't stop her from running toward Matt as he jogged into the intersection.

"Are you okay?" she asked. Her run was more of a gaited hobble. It took everything in her not to cry out. "Are you hurt?" She didn't wait for an answer, giving him a once-over until her eyes caught on his leg. Blood stained his pants at the side of his thigh. "Matt!"

The detective reached out, wrapping his hands around her upper arms. He was steadying her, something she realized she needed.

"It's a graze," he answered, making sure to bring her eyes back up to his. "I'm fine. I promise. Has anyone called the police?"

Maggie nodded. It hurt.

"Jerry did when he drove up." She pointed back to the older man whom Maggie had yelled at to get into his car. He was now out of said car, trying to console a pregnant woman who had run to them. Maggie had already confirmed the expectant mother, Lea, was physically fine but understandably terrified. "What happened to the man?"

Anger squeezed his face. Maggie had to shut her eye as blood stung it again. Matt didn't miss it. He released her arms and grabbed the bottom of his shirt. With one quick movement he ripped off a strip.

"Here, use this," he offered. "It's still wet from the pool."

Maggie took the strip and ran it over her eye while Matt surprised her again by running his thumb across the skin between the cut and her eyebrow. When he pulled his finger away it was covered in blood.

"We need to get you out of here," he said, concern clear in his voice. It resonated within Maggie more than it should have. "Let's see if Jerry doesn't mind you using his car to rest until first responders get here."

Maggie didn't want to but she had to agree.

"Can I stay right here instead?" She looked down at her leg. Now that the adrenaline was starting to wear off, it was really starting to throb. "I—well, I just hurt."

"We need to get out of the open, just in case he comes back." Without saying anything more he put one arm behind her and then bent to put the other under her legs. One moment she was standing and the next she was in the detective's arms.

"Never thought Matt Walker would sweep me off my feet," she joked, trying to ignore how her eyes watered as the ache in her leg lessened but the one that reminded her she'd been in a car accident came to the forefront.

"It's been one heck of a day," Matt agreed. He walked them over to where Jerry and the woman were standing. "Jerry, is it? Why don't we let the ladies take a seat in your car while we wait?"

Jerry zipped to attention like Matt was a drill sergeant. Maggie half expected him to salute before he went about helping Lea into the back of the car. Matt stopped next to the other side and let her down gently.

Maggie kept her arm around his neck longer than was necessary, she was sure, but being so close to him—both wet and bleeding—something in her shifted.

"Thank you."

His eyebrow quirked up.

"For what?" he returned, voice low and filling with anger. "I let him get away. Again."

Maggie didn't have to force her sarcasm to stay away. She meant every word before she said it.

"For trying to save me at the hotel." Maggie was whispering now. "And for waking up when I called for you." She pulled her arm from around him but stayed close. "After the crash, when everything stopped moving—" Maggie paused as she felt the same panic again. Tears pricked the insides of her eyes. She didn't know where the emotion was coming from but she didn't try to fight it. "You stopped moving, too. He pulled me out before I could check to make sure you were—" Maggie cut her words off. She gave him a small, grateful smile. "Thank you for waking up."

Matt didn't return the smile but he answered her in a matching whisper. Like they were sharing secrets in their own little bubble.

"All thanks go to you," he said. "You're what woke me up."

Just like that Maggie's attention changed directions. From trying to cobble together a thank-you to her savior to glancing at his lips so close to hers, her aching body betrayed her mind. In that moment Maggie knew exactly what the new feeling was that swept through her.

She wanted to kiss Detective Matt Walker.

Because he'd tried to and actually had saved her. Because her breath had caught when he'd run into danger and her body had sagged in relief when he'd come back alive. Because he was the most handsome man she'd ever met. Because Maggie just wanted to feel his lips against hers.

Period.

But what did Matt want? Her? Or had she truly burned that bridge years ago?

Sirens sounded in the distance.

It burst their private bubble.

Matt reached around her and opened the car door. He remained gentle as he helped her into the seat. Then he rejoined Jerry outside at the front of the car.

He never met her eyes.

"KNOCK, KNOCK."

Maggie looked up from the magazine she'd been pretending to read and was surprised to see a familiar face.

"Nurse Bean," she started, then corrected herself. "Kortnie, I mean."

The ER nurse nodded with a smile. She was wearing her scrubs but her name tag was off. She thumbed at the spot it had been clipped to the night before.

"I just finished a double," she explained. "Was on my way out the door when I heard another fuss being kicked up with your name in the center. I have to admit I was hoping I wouldn't see you again. At least, not this quickly."

Maggie raised her hands in defense.

"I swear I'm not doing this on purpose. Trouble seems to be my middle name as of late is all."

Maggie had been ordered to go to the hospital as soon as the first local police officer had shown up on the scene. Once she'd finally been able to see herself in a mirror, she'd realized why. She looked like she'd been dropped into a blender with some rocks thrown in for good measure. Blood and cuts and the weight of pain had created a startling image. Matt wasn't much better. She had a sneaking suspicion that he would have refused the ambulance had she not been around, staying at the crime scene until the sheriff arrived. Instead, he'd sat in the back of the ambulance with Maggie as the EMT rattled off a series of questions.

Now, two hours later, and Maggie had been left in a room to wait for Matt's meeting with the sheriff to come to an end. They were down the hall. Both refused to go any farther than that, considering their mystery man had shown up twice in one day.

Kortnie walked in with a chart, head bent and ready to read it but Maggie beat her to it. She pointed to the cut above her eyebrow.

"It bled a lot but was superficial. No stitches, thank goodness, because I already look like a disaster. I might have a small scar, though." She pointed down to her leg raised up on the bed. "Pulled a muscle. I'm supposed to take it easy for a few days. Or a week. But who has time for that?" Maggie motioned to her body as a whole. "And last but not least, bruising plus the occasional laceration."

Kortnie smirked and crossed her arms over her chest.

"And the old noggin?"

Maggie sighed. It still hurt.

"I'm not missing any more memories," she said. "But I didn't remember anything from yesterday, either."

"Even still, let's hope you can avoid any more traumatic events, okay?"

Maggie shrugged.

"I'll really try. I promise. Maybe."

Kortnie laughed and the two dived into small talk that surprisingly wasn't forced. Maggie didn't have the best track record with female friends so the company was unexpected but pleasant. Maggie brought up Cody and how she missed him despite seeing him that morning which turned into Kortnie bringing up her own son. From there they talked about their respective jobs and were about to get into the politics behind PTA when Maggie was reminded that her life had become more complicated than normal. Matt walked in looking more world-weary than he had that morning.

"And that's my cue to go home and sleep," Kortnie said before the detective could ask for some privacy. She rummaged through her purse and pulled out a card. "On the off chance trouble finds you for a third time today," she said, handing the card over, "I was a hospital administrator before I switched back to my nursing roots and the ER but my number is still the same."

Maggie smiled at the thought.

"Thanks. I'd give you one in return but, to be honest, I have no idea where my purse is right now." Her tone let Kortnie know it was okay to laugh and soon the nurse was saying goodbye. Matt didn't talk until the door shut behind her.

"I chased down your doctor," he started, sinking into the chair next to the bed. "We can leave when you're ready." His eyes went to her leg but he kept quiet about it. He hadn't left her side until she'd been checked out when they had first come in. Which meant he knew she'd been asked to keep off it. There was no point lying.

"It hurts but not as bad as it did. The medicine for inflammation helped."

He nodded. He looked lost. Tired.

"Matt, what did the sheriff say?"

The detective ran his hand down his face.

"The APB is still out for our perp and this time we know what he looks like and the exact make and model of the car he took so that should help. Local PD are coordinating with the sheriff's department to work every angle available to try to get this guy. They're retracing *our* steps to see if anyone saw anything helpful, and Detective Ansler is probably dissecting the truck as we speak." He opened his mouth and then closed it.

"What?" she prodded.

"Something our mystery man said is bothering me. He said he didn't kill women."

Maggie felt her eyebrow rise.

"Last time I checked that was a good thing."

Matt gave her a dry look.

"It is. *But* it was the way he said it that was off." He sat up straighter. "Like he was saying *he* didn't kill women but—"

"But someone else did," she interrupted.

He nodded.

"There's already so much about this man we don't

know. Can you imagine if we were really dealing with *two* people?"

A shiver ran up Maggie's spine at even the hint of more than one bad guy who wanted to keep whatever secret she'd uncovered a secret. Especially when the maybe accomplice wasn't above killing women.

"Hey, either way," Matt said, scooting to the edge of his chair, "you solved this thing once already. There's no reason we can't do it again."

Maggie couldn't help but smirk at that.

"Every time we team up, a man in a van or truck appears," she pointed out. "Maybe we should table our investigation until we at least get some better pain meds."

The detective snorted and, once again, ran his hand down his face. It worried her.

"Billy is going to take us to the hotel where we're going to lie low for a while. I've been officially benched and *I'm* officially benching you. I should remind you the doctor will back me up on this."

Maggie rewound and settled on the first part.

"We? I thought Deputy Foster was being assigned to watch Cody and me?"

"He is but, while I trust him, I don't think he can handle you on his own." A small smirk crossed his lips but a smirk nonetheless. It made their darkening conversation brighten a moment.

"You act like I'm some wild creature. The past few days are not an entirely accurate representation of my life."

He snorted.

"The past few days might not be your normal speed but in just one morning I've been witness to you wanting to chase a man who threw bricks into your home, strip in public to retrieve a clue you *hid at the bottom of a hotel pool* and break out of a gunman's grip with ease after riding out a crash that was like being tossed in the spin cycle. Yeah, I don't think I can accurately warn Caleb what you're capable of." He got to his feet. It was a labored move. She'd overheard the nurse chastise him about moving around so much. His ribs weren't broken but they were bruised. And had been already when he'd carried Maggie across the intersection, worsening his pain to help alleviate hers. In the same gentlemanly fashion, he held his hand out to her now.

"But I thought you were benched," she added, hesitating from taking it. "You know, since you're hurt and haven't slept in a few days and people tend to need rest."

"Billy can bench me all day long but what I do in my spare time is my business. Now, you want to get out of here or what?"

Chapter Thirteen

The hotel was definitely a step up from the one Luca was running. That was for sure. Maggie followed Matt and Sheriff Reed up to the third floor where they'd already booked a room for her and Cody. It was nice and not too small. There were two double beds, a love seat and a TV. The view from the window showed the top of an office complex next door and, if you knew just where to look and squinted, you could just make out the corner of the Riker County Sheriff's Department.

The building's proximity did little in the way of easing any part of Matt's or the sheriff's minds. They spoke to one another, quickly and quietly, heads bent together, while Maggie unpacked the bag she'd made for her and Cody. A little less chaos was what she needed right now. She even took out his favorite books and toys and positioned them on one of the beds, hoping that their presence would make the fact they were in a hotel room and not home a little less jarring.

"I'm going to go to the school now, Ms. Carson," the sheriff said just as Maggie was putting her clothes in the dresser. "After everything that's happened I want to provide extra backup for Cody, just in case."

Maggie nodded.

"I won't argue with that."

"Good. I'll give you a call once I get to the school to let you know we're on the way back." The sheriff turned to Matt. "Deputy Foster should be here in a few minutes with a bag from your place."

Matt's eyebrow rose. Sheriff Reed held up his hand to stop him.

"I don't have to be a detective to know you've already made up your mind about sticking around," he said. "Which is why I also booked the adjoining room for you."

They turned to the door next to the dresser.

"Deputies Mills and Grayson came out here earlier to check everything out," he continued. He pulled a key out of his pocket and handed it over. "It's technically two doors so if you want to open it, you each have to use your own key to do so."

Maggie watched as the detective's expression turned to one of appreciation. She couldn't help but mimic the feeling. Having Matt close by was one of the few thoughts that made her feel more secure.

"Let me know if you need anything," the sheriff said, already walking to the door. "Try to rest while you can. *Both* of you. I'll call you as soon as I get to the school."

Maggie thanked the man and shut the door behind him.

Leaving her alone with Matt.

In a hotel room.

Oh, how strange this day was.

"Well, I don't know about you, but I think I need to get a quick shower so I don't have to explain to my son why I look like a zombie and smell like a pool."

Matt beat her to the bathroom, turned on the light and did a quick search. It was unnecessary, she believed, but touching.

"Do you mind if I keep the adjoining door open until Caleb gets here?" he asked, unaware that he'd unintentionally ignited a bit of heat within her. "I'd rather not break down all of these doors if something happens."

Maggie laughed and tossed him the key card the sheriff had given her.

"I'd rather we not break anything else today if possible," she said. "I still feel really bad about the Bronco. Even if we didn't ask to be bulldozed by some deranged stranger."

Matt caught the key and went to open both of the doors. It was like looking into a mirror, an identical room reflected back beyond it. He put her key on the dresser and paused in the doorway.

"Are you okay for now?"

His eyes went to the lone crutch beneath her arm. She waved him off.

"Nothing I can't handle," she assured him. "But,

Matt, maybe after the deputy gets here you should think about taking a nice long shower." She cracked a grin. "I also don't want to explain to my son why the normally good-looking detective looks like he's visited the inside of a blender and *also* smells like he's switched his cologne for chlorine."

Matt smirked.

"I'm going to take the compliment of 'good-looking' away from that and move on."

A little bit of heat crawled up Maggie's neck. She hadn't realized she said he was good-looking.

Although, she wasn't about to take it back, either.

THE SHOWER MIGHT have been difficult to navigate since almost every part of her body was hurting, but Maggie couldn't deny that the hot water pelting her felt amazing. However, when it was time to dress herself she encountered more of a problem.

Pulling her hair up in a loose, wet bun, she shimmied into her bra, blouse and panties. Then, with a little more trepidation than she was used to feeling, she cracked the bathroom door open.

"Uh, Detective?"

She pressed her face against the inside of the door until she heard movement.

"Yeah? Is everything okay?"

Maggie felt the blush before the heat ever reached her skin.

"Yeah," she called back, clearing her throat. "Are you alone by chance?"

There was a pause.

"I am."

Maggie took a small breath.

"And we're both adult enough to admit you've seen me in my underwear already, right? And we were both really professional about it?"

The pause was longer this time.

"Matt?"

"Yeah," he replied. "What are you getting at?"

With her free hand Maggie finagled the crutch beneath her arm and opened the door all the way. She held her chin high as she walked out into the middle of the room, nothing but her blouse and a pair of black panties on.

"Now, before you think I just like showing you my unmentionables," she said quickly, stopping at the foot of the closest bed, "I want to remind you that I've been in the ER twice in twenty-four hours and my body has finally decided to let me know how much it dislikes that. It stages its own little protest every time I try to put on my pants."

Matt's eyes stayed on hers as she spoke. Like she was the most interesting woman in the world and every syllable was as good as a tied football game in the fourth quarter. When, really, he just didn't want to look down. Maggie didn't know if she should be offended or not.

"The medicine they gave you isn't helping?"

Maggie shrugged.

"Yes and no. I mean I'm not feeling like I'm going

to be sick when I move but everything feels stiff and uncomfortable." She gave him a look that she hoped expressed just how much she'd love for him to agree to help her put on skinny jeans.

He sighed.

"All right. Are they in the bathroom, then?"

Maggie nodded and laid her crutch on the bed. She remained standing until Matt was in front of her. He crouched down and Maggie felt a flame ignite just south of her waistline as he passed her panties. Apparently, she wasn't the only one. A glance down showed the detective's face was as red as a cherry. Which was a sight in itself. Even his ears were turning scarlet.

"Never thought I'd see Matt Walker blush," Maggie couldn't help but say. What was the point of being quiet if the situation would have still been just as strange as it was with no talking? "It's like you've never been asked to help a girl get dressed before."

The man was holding her jeans like a matador holding a red flag. That made her the bull in the scenario but it was the only image she could imagine, looking at the detective's expression when he met her gaze.

Caution.

Suspicion.

Focus.

And a dash of cockiness.

"When it comes to women, I've only ever been asked to help take clothes *off*."

Maggie's blush seared across her skin. It didn't help that the back of his hand skimmed the side of her leg as he tried to steady her. Good thing she'd been able to put on her shirt. The two of them might have been stained tomato red otherwise.

"Now, hold on to me," Matt ordered. "Last thing we need is you falling over and earning us a one-way trip right back to the hospital. Three times in twenty-four hours might get you thrown in a padded room somewhere. Just so you don't hurt yourself."

Maggie laughed and followed Matt's command with little to no grace. She held on to his shoulders as he navigated one pant leg halfway up and then moved to the other one to do the same. The pain wasn't as bad as it had been thanks to the lingering medicine from the hospital but when she'd stepped out of the shower and tried to work the material around her bad leg, she'd been met with surprising resistance. It was like her entire leg had been frozen stiff, refusing to bend with her.

She hadn't thought to involve the detective until three attempts ended with the rest of her body reminding her it had been beaten up, too. Now the dull throb that blanketed her was only being interrupted by the burn of her blush…and something else. It wasn't a mystery what that other thing was, either. Every time Matt's skin came in contact with hers, no matter how innocent, it was like he was lighting matches along her body. Trailing them from one spot to the other until it went out and he struck up another one. The detective was touching parts of her skin that hadn't been touched by a man in a long time.

It completely distracted her to the point he had to repeat himself.

"Lift your other leg," he said. "Unless you want to explain to Cody why you can't do it yourself."

Maggie cleared her throat. The longing for the man at her feet quieted as her thoughts moved to her son.

"While he's mature for his age I *would* like to avoid that particular conversation," she admitted. "He's already been through enough in his young life. I'd like to keep him a kid as long as possible."

She winced as she put weight on her bad ankle for a second. Matt looped the pant leg under her foot as fast and gently as he could. He pulled up until it slid to above her knee.

"You got it from here?"

Maggie nodded. She grabbed the waist of her jeans as he turned away to give her privacy to pull them the rest of the way up and button them. Not that it was needed. He'd already seen her.

"And who said chivalry is dead?" she joked, lowering herself onto the bed when she was done.

Matt snorted and walked over to the window. He moved the curtains back, letting light stream through. It lit up his hair.

Golden.

Beautiful.

Worthy of a pair of hands running through it.

The cut above her eyebrow stung.

Maggie sighed.

All jokes and sarcasm aside, she couldn't ignore how horrible she felt. Which had to mean that her steadfast companion must have felt worse. He had, after all, not slept in nearly two days as far as she knew.

It was a painful reminder that one man had put them through the ringer within the span of one morning. Suddenly, she didn't feel so jovial.

"Did you know I was married before all of this happened? I mean before I told you I'd been divorced?" The question surprised her. Matt turned to listen. But to what? She wasn't sure. In a flash she went from feeling lust and humor to something much more dangerous. Overwhelming vulnerability.

"No," he answered stoically. "I didn't."

Maggie exhaled a long breath.

"I interviewed him when I first started working at the paper in Kipsy. It was some fluff piece about a diner being renovated after fifty years of serving the community. Chris was a lawyer, family law, but loved the diner so much that every Wednesday he'd go to work an hour early so he'd have a longer lunch break to fit the extra twenty-minute commute." Maggie felt herself smile a little. She knew it was broken. All the happy memories of her ex were still there, in her heart, but just off enough that reliving them brought a twinge of pain. "He loved that place," she continued. "And that's where he told me he loved me. He asked me to marry him in the booth we sat in during that first interview. I know it sounds cheesy but at the time it was perfect. *We* were perfect."

Maggie brought her hands up to help illustrate a point she'd already made to herself in the past several years. She laced her fingers together, pushing her palms flush.

"We fit together like this—so snug, so great—but as time went on, I realized that this—" she shook her clasped hands "—this isn't perfect. Because, if you look down, you'll see that one of the two hands is on top. One thumb over the other. Not equal. Not in sync. No matter how great it might look at first."

Maggie let her hands fall to her lap.

"I didn't realize that our marriage wasn't the way it should have been until life really started happening. I may have been—and still am—difficult and aggressive and intrusive and a list of other adjectives that you'd use to define people who usually end up alone, but even I, with all my flaws, thought I deserved to try to be happy. And that *desire* ended up eating its way through my chest and then into other parts of my life until I had nothing left to distract me from it." She gave him an apologetic look. "Becoming, for lack of a better word, obsessed with cases and stories that I had no business getting attached to, for instance."

Matt kept quiet. Which was fine. For some reason Maggie realized she needed to get some things off her chest.

"Adopting Cody, I can see now, wasn't about just saving him. It was about saving me, too." Tears began to prick the insides of her eyes but Maggie didn't stop. Not when she was so close to making her point. "See, I come from a small family. Two parents, an idiot brother who does idiot things and an aunt I saw once a year until she remarried and moved across the ocean. They loved me, my family, but in a detached way. Not the most involved bunch but they call on birthdays and holidays and even sometimes try to fit a visit into their schedule. It's just who they are and have always been. It's how I grew up. I can't fault them because I had a good, healthy childhood. We loved each other but... Well, we weren't *a team* like so many other families seem to be." Maggie felt her lips pull up for a moment. "The first month Cody lived with Chris and me, he got sick. You know, I knew what you were supposed to do when your kid gets sick. Take them to the doctor, give them the medicine, watch over the kid until they're better. But things in theory are always easier, aren't they? At first I was doing fine, sticking by the book on how to help him. But one time when I touched his cheek to see how hot he was, he looked up at me with these round, innocent eyes, and I swear I felt that fever in my bones."

Maggie knew why the vulnerability was there and why she had felt the need to tell the man a few feet from her everything. Why she wasn't the same woman he'd met years ago. Why she'd really put the case away. Why she needed them to solve it now.

"It was in that moment that I knew I *finally* had a team." She smiled and felt the tears slide down her face. She didn't care. She wanted him to know the bottom line. "We can't let anything happen to that boy, Matt. He's my entire life and then some. We have to finish this thing. Whatever it is."

The detective stayed right where he was but that didn't lessen the severity of his response. Despite the distance between them she felt as if he was close enough to kiss.

"We might have been banged up today, Maggie, but I promise you, Cody will never be hurt." His voice was steel. "And just because this case is difficult doesn't mean it's impossible. I believe in the sheriff, the department and even local PD." A smile carved itself out of his frown. It was small but effective. "I even believe in us."

Maggie didn't bother wiping at her cheek. She felt a surge of relief wash over all the pain and doubt and worry. It might not last but she welcomed it.

And was thankful for the man who had given it to her.

She smiled.

"You better be careful, Detective. You keep talking like that and I'll start to think you actually like me."

Matt snorted.

"Well, we wouldn't want that."

Those blue-gray eyes found hers.

"No, we wouldn't want that."

Chapter Fourteen

Maggie might have started to cry when she opened up to him, but when Cody finally arrived she managed to hold it together remarkably well. However, she wasted no time in wrapping him in her arms as if he were a life preserver in choppy waters. Cody, more curious about their new surroundings, returned the hug. Then squirmed when Maggie had a hard time letting go.

"Mom," he whined. "You're crushing me!"

Maggie laughed but didn't pull away until she gave one more squeeze. She looked up when she was done and met Matt's gaze through the open adjoining room door.

"I finally had a team."

Matt broke the stare and let Maggie's words echo one last time through his head as he took his bag to the bathroom to shower and change. He tried to coax his mind into going blank so he could enjoy the quiet, especially after everything that had happened.

Everything he thought he'd known. Everything he'd learned. But the thoughts came hard and fast.

Ken Morrison might have killed Erin because of their mystery man with a moral code that included not killing women.

But why? What was the point? And what did it have to do with the list of names Maggie had found?

Matt let the hot water run across his face and down his body.

Erin.

The ache of loss started to spread. His fists balled. He'd already done this. He'd already fallen apart, felt destroyed and lost. He'd already done the horrible dance of burying a loved one. A wife.

It was hard but he'd tried his best to move on. He'd grieved. He still did in his own way when he was reminded of the once-little things that seemed so big and empty now. Whether it was the side of the bed that remained cold, the fact that the shampoo and soap in the shower were only his, or the at times startling realization that he'd never again see her use the chipped New Orleans mug he'd bought her on their honeymoon, Matt had tried his best to heal the ache. Or at least embrace it until it eased.

Now, though, how could he do what he always had if Erin's death had been intentional?

Matt opened his hands. Thinking of Maggie, he pressed them together without lacing his fingers.

Equal. In sync.

They'd both lost someone they had hoped would be a partner for life.

Matt sighed into the steam.

The weight of exhaustion was finally starting to crush him. He finished his shower, dressed and sat down for the first time in what felt like days. The door between their rooms remained open.

Matt fell asleep to the sounds of laughter between mother and son.

IT WAS SOMEWHERE between dreams and reality that an answer found its way into Matt's head. He opened his eyes, blinking the sleep away, and felt a wave of disorientation. A dim light was in the distance but everything in his immediate area was dark. For a moment he forgot where he was and a sense of panic seized him.

A noise followed by subtle movement at his side turned that panic into action. He reached out and caught someone's wrist. They tried to resist and soon he felt the weight of a body on his.

"What the heck, Matt?"

The voice and body pressed on top of his belonged to Maggie. He took a deep breath, trying to calm his racing heart, and reached out toward the lamp on the nightstand. He remembered now where he was. But couldn't imagine why Maggie was on top of him.

The light wasn't great but it showed him a red-faced woman struggling to roll off him. It was distracting to say the least. Here he was trying to concentrate on reorienting himself and instead all he could seem to focus on was the heat of Maggie's body pressed against him. Her curves and softness. Moving against him.

As swiftly as she'd fallen over, Matt realized he needed to focus on anything other than the woman or else she would know exactly what he thought of her body. What *his* body thought of her body.

"Maggie," he whispered through gritted teeth. "Just roll over."

"You act like that's *easy* with the list of injuries and pain meds," she bit back, sounding as irritated as he did. Though he doubted she was fighting her body's responses as hard as he was at the moment. "Walking like five steps over here was difficult enough."

Matt grunted to no one in particular and decided to move the woman himself. He tried to sit up and roll her over on her back next to him. His body went from registering desire to handling a wallop of pain. He winced but followed through on his original plan until Maggie was lying in the bed next to him instead of on top of him.

For a moment they were quiet, both catching their breath and waiting for their various pains to ebb.

Maggie was the one who broke the silence.

"Well, I can't say that's how I imagined getting you into bed." There was the normal Maggie snark in her tone.

"You always have a response for something. Do you realize that?"

They both kept their gazes to the ceiling. Still, he saw her shrug.

"I do what I can."

"And what exactly were you doing just now?" he asked. "Before you fell over onto me."

"To be fair, you scared me so the falling part is on you." Her voice softened. "But originally, I came in to check up on you. You've been asleep for a while now."

Matt grabbed at his side and fought through the pain to grab his phone off the nightstand. It was a quarter after nine.

"Honestly, I think you need *more* sleep," she said. "I just wanted to make sure you were all right. But I guess it's hard to sneak around with a crutch. Sorry I woke you."

There were no missed calls or texts on his phone. Which meant there had been no breaks in the case while he'd been asleep. It was frustrating, to say the least.

"Is Caleb still outside?" he asked. He'd been so tired he'd barely spoken to the deputy earlier.

She nodded.

"I let him know when I was putting Cody to bed. I gave him a stern, motherly warning to not disturb us unless something big happened." She flashed him a smirk. "And even then be quiet about it. If there's one thing I'm proud of about my kid, it's that he sleeps hard. But Heaven help us if he *does* wake up. I'm

pretty sure I've learned the skills of an expert nego-
tiator because of that boy."

Matt smiled and shifted his gaze until he saw
Cody's sleeping form through the open door. His
mouth was open and his arm was hanging halfway
off the bed.

"I envy how easily kids can sleep," he admitted.
"The older we get the harder it becomes."

He hadn't meant to take the conversation down
a more serious path but suddenly it felt like he had.
Silence moved between them until Maggie let out a
breath that dragged down her body, despite the fact
she was already lying down.

"It's because we know the truth about nightmares,"
she whispered. "They can be all too real."

Matt angled his head to get a better look at the
woman. Green eyes met his. Within them a nearly
imperceptible shift happened.

The two of them whispering in the dark suddenly
felt right. Them, so close together he could still feel
the warmth of her body, felt right.

Matt glanced down at Maggie's lips.

Suddenly, he felt like the two of them hadn't just
been trying to solve a mystery all day but also building toward something.

"Maggie," he started but she didn't let him finish.

With an almost-apologetic smile she pulled herself up until she was sitting with her back against the
headrest. He could tell the movement was painful but
she didn't complain.

"Sorry again for waking you up. But now that I know you're alive and well, I think it's time I made the long trek back to my room."

The moment, whatever it was, dissipated.

Maggie was back to being the woman who had found herself in the middle of trouble.

And he was back to being the detective who needed to figure out who was behind it all.

IT WASN'T UNTIL he awoke the next morning that Matt remembered what his dream had told him the night before. A part of him wished Maggie was still in bed with him. Rolling over to tell her his theory would have been a lot less painful.

He felt like he'd been hit by a truck. Well, he really had been. The side of his body was an ache he couldn't escape. One that whined as he tried the simplest of tasks. Never mind his ribs. The doctor had confirmed they had been bruised. The adrenaline had masked that particular nuisance after the crash but now there was nothing dulling it. Apparently, Maggie was having the same issues.

He looked through the open door between them after he finished changing and caught her eye. She was sitting up in bed, her foot propped up on some pillows.

"*Not being broken* isn't the same as *feeling okay*," she called. "At least if something's broken, they give you more pain medication." Her brow was furrowed. She uncrossed her arms to wave him in. The bed next to her was disheveled but empty. The bathroom door was open but empty. She followed his gaze to it. "Cody's in the hallway talking Deputy Foster's ear off. I didn't want Cody to go to school, considering Brick Thrower made a point to let us know that he's familiar with my life. On the off chance he still wants me after getting that key, I don't want to give him the opportunity to grab my son."

"Speaking of the key, I realized something about it."

Maggie's entire body perked up.

"Yeah? What?"

"It was a small key, right? Probably to a lock?"

Maggie nodded.

"And what do people nowadays really use those for?"

"Other than bikes and maybe the occasional shed, I don't know."

A thread of excitement started to wrap itself around Matt's gut. The idea of a lead, no matter how theorized, was one of the best parts about his job. It pushed them closer to the truth, to completing the puzzle.

"Storage units," he answered. "You rent a unit and bring your own lock."

Maggie's eyes widened. Then she was smiling right along with him, catching on to his excitement. However, it didn't last.

"But whose storage unit would it go to? And why would that guy yesterday want it?"

Matt had already had the same questions. He pointed to her.

"I don't know but *you* did at some point. Why else would you have hidden it?"

"The operative word is *did*," she pointed out. "Now? Not so much."

"If you could figure it out once, you can do it again."

The hotel door opened. Cody walked in, looking thoughtful. Deputy Foster nodded to Matt before shutting the door behind the boy. When Cody saw Matt he hesitated.

"Cody, you remember Detective Walker?"

The boy's eyes were wide. Such acute concern seemed to cross his face that Matt felt his face draw in, too.

"You got hurt like Mom," the boy said. "You have cuts on your face."

Matt had forgotten that beyond feeling bad, he also looked it. Maggie, on the other hand, had lessened the intensity of her appearance with makeup. But no amount could cover up everything. Matt wished he'd thought to ask Maggie how she'd explained what had happened to the boy.

"I did," he decided to tell the truth. "But it's not that bad."

Cody looked him up and down. Then he nodded, apparently accepting Matt's statement as truth.

"Okay." The boy turned to Maggie. "Mom, I'm hungry."

Maggie laughed. She shared a look with Matt.

"He really does care," she promised. "Just not a lot until he gets some food."

Matt put his hands on his waist and turned back to the boy, serious.

"Well, I can't blame him. Us men need nourishment."

Cody nodded, mimicking Matt's stern expression. "Yeah, Mom."

Maggie held her hands up.

"I guess I can't argue with that logic."

Chapter Fifteen

It wasn't until Tuesday afternoon that something shook loose with the case. By that time it had been four days of hotel living. Four days of fast food and room service. Four days of being cooped up and slowly going stir-crazy. Four days of forced proximity with a man Maggie had spent five years avoiding.

The first day Matt had kept his distance after breakfast. He'd kept the door open between their rooms but worked on his laptop and phone, out of sight at his desk. The only conversation she'd heard was him checking on Dwayne's condition at the hospital. Maggie had tried to eavesdrop on more of his calls, or when Sheriff Reed or Detective Ansler had stopped by, but Cody had made that difficult. It was like she had a toddler all over again. His books, toys and the television did little to ease his restlessness. It wasn't until day two that Matt was able to ease some of the pressure.

"Want to explore the hotel for a few minutes with me?" he asked after they finished off their lunch at the lone table in her room. "I was thinking about stretching my legs."

Cody had lit up like a Christmas tree. He was still working through his shyness with Matt but the offer had been too good for him to stay silent. His little eyes found their way to hers and he'd started in with a chorus of "Please, Mom" and "Pretty please."

Matt's "I won't let him out of my sight" was what really did the trick.

The two had marched out of the hotel room with purpose and they'd come back in with smiles. Apparently, Matt had regaled the boy with watered-down police stories full of action and mystery. So much so that they'd taken another walk that night—and every day since. It became a little ritual, one Maggie couldn't join in on.

While she was itching to stretch her own legs or to track down and follow any bread crumbs that could lead to lost memories, Maggie was grateful for the break. Her leg, along with all the other postaccident pain, had been given time to heal. Or at least get to the point where mobility without cringing was possible.

She'd used the downtime to drag out her own laptop—grabbed by the sheriff and his wife, who had offered to pick up extra clothes for her and Matt and Cody—and revisited her original investigation into Erin Walker's death. Afterward, she'd made a list of everything they knew from recent events. Including his interest in the key she'd hidden at the hotel. Following Matt's theory that it could belong to a storage unit had focused her attention on the several in Kipsy and the rest of the county. She'd stared at the new and old information until her eyes crossed. Until she felt like she was going crazy. Nothing was adding up. Not *one* damn thing.

That is until Tuesday afternoon when a news story popped up on the *Kipsy City Chronicle*'s Facebook page. It was a link to their crime blog but it was the caption that made Maggie stop scrolling.

The Kipsy Police Department is asking for the public's help in finding a suspect in a recent break-in at a local storage-unit facility.

Maggie clicked the link, heartbeat already speeding up. A picture of a Danny's Storage Facility billboard was at the top of the page. The press release beneath it was short. However, it was enough to get Maggie going. She grabbed the pen and hotel notepad and scribbled down Danny's Storage Facility's address. When she was done with that, she focused on her leg.

The swelling had gone down but there was still some soreness. She'd spent the past few days testing the limits of her mobility and could, at the very least, walk without her crutch. It just hurt a little and was less of a walk and more of a limp.

Now she tested her leg again, moving around the room in search of socks and shoes and lipstick. The lipstick wasn't necessary but Maggie still grabbed the tube and put it on with conviction. She was excited and wanted Matt to get on the same wavelength. Plus, she hoped putting on lipstick showed him without her having to say it that she meant business. Maggie straightened her back, held the piece of paper in her hand like it was the track-and-field baton and waited to pass it off to the detective the moment he came through the door.

Luckily, she didn't have to wait long.

"We saw a squirrel jump off the roof," sang Cody, riding his own wave of excitement into the room. Maggie paused only long enough to get an explanation for that.

"One of the rooms was open and we scoped it out," Matt jumped in. "Through the window we saw a squirrel jump off the roof next door onto a tree."

Cody made a stretched-out scoff.

"That's what I *just* said!"

Matt laughed and held up his hands in defense.

Maggie used the opening to push the paper into the palm of one of them. It confused the detective but he read it regardless.

"And this is?"

Maggie was brimming with excitement now. It showed her how stir-crazy she'd actually become being cooped up in their two rooms for days.

"Cody, why don't you go see what's on Matt's TV?" she answered instead. "Channel 14 has an all-day marathon of *Bill Nye the Science Guy*."

Maggie didn't have to tell the boy twice. He was

already singing the theme song before he even made it through the adjoining room's door. Matt, however, was waiting with his eyebrow raised.

"That's the address to a storage-unit facility in Kipsy," she started. "There was a break-in, but they don't have any leads as to who was behind it."

It was as if someone had sprinkled Miracle-Gro over the man. He perked right up.

"This could be our guy."

Maggie nodded but held up her index finger to keep his attention.

"*But* the break-in happened *last week*," she corrected. "They just didn't catch it until this morning."

His eyes widened.

"So barring coincidence, this break-in could have been—"

Maggie couldn't help herself. She cut him off.

"Me! It could have been me. The timing lines up with my missing chunk of memory. I hid the key before lunch in the hotel room. So maybe I took Cody to school and went to the storage unit afterward. Then took the key with me to meet whoever gave me that card for the hotel but then I, for whatever reason, felt the need to hide it. And well…"

"But why? What did you find that led you to the key in the first place? And when did you leave your house without your purse or keys?"

Maggie's thread of excitement began to unravel.

"I don't know," she admitted with a shrug. "But that storage unit may or may not hold the answer."

Matt eyeballed the address again.

"Did you tell anyone else about this?"

"No. Just you."

He ran his hand through his hair.

"I need to call Billy. Get someone out there."

Maggie held her hands up in a stopping motion.

"*Or*, hear me out," she said. "*We*, me and you, go check it out first and let them keep following whatever leads they're following."

Matt raised his eyebrow and snorted.

"I'm not about to welcome trouble by walking straight into it. That's not good police business, or any business really."

"But we don't even know where our mystery perp is," she pointed out. "Last time we saw him, you shot him. There's a good chance he's long gone or at least lying low." Maggie swept her arm backward, motioning to the room as a whole. "As much as I've enjoyed our nose-to-the-grindstone, operating-out-of-a-hotel-room methods of investigation, we haven't gotten anywhere in days. Neither have the rest of the department or the local police. And again, as much as I've enjoyed our nonangry meals and our nightly game show viewing, we can't stay in this hotel forever." Maggie lowered her voice, hoping Matt caught her shift from optimistic to the direct opposite. "Eventually, we'll all have to go home. Our separate homes. But right now *this* is the only lead we have. And I want—need—to see it for myself. To see if any of it is a missing piece to what I did during the span of one lousy day." Matt kept his eyes on hers as she took a small step closer to him. "Please, Matt, I need to do this. Help me do this."

For one long moment Maggie was sure he'd say no. Then cite off all the reasons—all legitimate, too— that the two of them going back out into the field, busted and partially broken with a target on her back and a child hidden in a hotel room, was a no-good, very bad idea.

But he didn't.

Detective Matt Walker actually grinned.

"I think I've finally accepted the fact that you're just the most persistent pain in the backside I'll ever know."

Maggie felt herself beam. She placed a hand over her chest and upped her Southern accent to classic Scarlett O'Hara.

"Why, Detective, I do think that's just about the nicest thing I ever did hear."

DEPUTY FOSTER HAD been on guard duty every day since they'd first come to the hotel. His partner, Dante Mills, took the night shift so he wouldn't be run ragged. Though Matt almost wished the deputy was a little slow on his feet that afternoon. Because he might have swallowed their story a little easier. Instead, his eyebrows rode high and his questions swung low.

"And why can't we just send Detective Ansler out there?" he asked, circling back to his original objection of the two of them leaving.

Maggie opened her mouth to, no doubt, argue her points again, but Matt gave her a look that doused that particular flame. She let him do the talking, though he could tell she was ready to jump in at any moment she thought he was failing. So he decided not to fail.

"Listen, Caleb, there are lines," he started.

"Lines," the deputy repeated.

"Yeah, lines. There's a misconception about lines. On account of there's not just one of them," he continued. "There are tons of them. Boatloads of them. And they all separate *something you haven't done yet* from *something you shouldn't do at all*. The moment you cross any line, you can't go back. There's just another line now, in front of you, that you shouldn't cross, either. So in our line of work, it's important we don't cross the lines. And if we do, that we don't cross so many that we stop seeing the new ones that pop up." Matt squared his shoulders. He liked Caleb and didn't want to lie to him. So he was taking the direct approach, flowered by some blunt conversation. "In my career I've crossed a few. Ones that I didn't realize were even there until I'd jumped clear of them. And I know you can agree with me on that."

Caleb had more demons than most in his past. So he kept quiet on the point. He certainly couldn't dispute it.

"But I'm here to tell you right now that I know this is a line I'm crossing." He motioned to Maggie. "But it's worth it if we can finish this damned case. You just have to trust me on that."

Caleb looked between them. Matt wondered if he was thinking about the lines he'd crossed to help his now girlfriend, Alyssa, when she'd found herself with a wild target on her head, too. He'd had moments of going rogue in his tale to save the girl. And that was probably what helped him agree.

Though it took a few beats before he answered.

"Fine. But you gotta tell Billy. You need backup, no matter how good your intentions. You know the sheriff will argue but he won't stop you from going." Caleb grinned. "Especially if you give him that ridiculous speech you just gave me."

Matt snorted.

"Hey, I thought it was pretty eloquent myself."

"It was sure something," Maggie piped in. It made Caleb all out laugh.

"Okay, you two, get it all out," Matt said, waving them on. "We have serious work to do, so go ahead and get all of this mess out of your systems."

Maggie burrowed into a series of laughs before coming to a stop. She nodded. Caleb, too. It was a nice stress release, Matt realized. The three of them had been wound tight, ordered to stay on their toes for whatever attack may come. Matt also realized it would have been nice of him to talk to the deputy more during his posts.

"Thank you, Caleb," he said, sobering. "I know this hasn't been the most exciting detail."

The deputy fell back into his deputy composure.

"You don't hear me complaining," he assured.

"You two be careful. I'll make sure Cody stays safe." He said the last part to Maggie. "Only a few of us even know you're here. If we do get any trouble, though, I swear to you nothing will happen to him."

Maggie nodded, all traces of humor gone from her expression.

"Matt trusts you, so I trust you."

It was a simple statement but said with such basic honesty that Matt was taken aback.

Maggie didn't just trust him, she trusted his word. His instinct. On voucher alone she trusted a stranger to protect her child, her entire life, as she'd said earlier. A slow yet nearly overwhelming emotion started to slip into the detective's heart.

Pride?

No.

Gratefulness?

Not quite.

Affection?

Maggie found his gaze. Beautiful, trusting, determined eyes.

Qualities that easily described her, as well.

For days they had been trapped together within their rooms, connected by a door that had stayed mostly opened. Now, looking at a woman he used to loathe, Matt realized something had shifted between them in that time. Or, maybe, something had been building. Something they'd been trying to ignore or resist. Something unspoken.

Something coming to a head.

With every conversation, every wayward glance, every subtle touch, Matt had struggled to stay focused on the case and only the case. Instead he'd found his eyes straying to Maggie's lips, his thoughts hovering on her laughter, and his mind being filled with images of what could be between them.

It had been nearly impossible to stop.

It was distracting.

It was dangerous.

Yet, Matt couldn't help but wonder...

What would happen after the case was finished?

Chapter Sixteen

Danny's Storage Facility was near the city limits of Kipsy. It needed the room to stretch, taking up half an acre of indoor climate-controlled and outdoor non-climate-controlled units. No other businesses butted up against the place, but an old T-shirt press sat abandoned across the road.

Maggie wondered what kind of shirts they used to make as Matt drove their third car in a week up to the main office, the only building on the outside of a gate that closed in all the units. Matt's eyes were taking that gate in when he finally spoke.

"The buildings in front look brand-new," he noted, driving along the gate until they were in the parking lot. "How long did you say this place has been here?"

"At least a decade, I think." She pointed in the direction opposite them. "The article said they've recently been renovating. I assume out that way are the older units since you can't see them from the road. Still, there seems to be a lot of security here. At least around the gate."

Maggie tilted her head to the side, trying to size up what she would do to get inside, which would basically entail breaking and entering.

"I'd probably cut a hole in the fence before I'd attempt to climb that sucker," she said out loud. It earned her a questioning look from the detective. "I was just thinking about how I'd try to break in to this place. The answer would be cutting a hole somewhere in the fence. It looks like it's almost eight feet tall. No way I'd climb that. I may be fearless but I'm not stupid. My clumsy self would fall and break something."

Matt laughed and joined her looking out the windshield at the tall compound-like fence.

"But why would you break in if you have the key?" he pointed out.

"Maybe I wasn't supposed to have the key in the first place?"

Matt sighed and started to get out of the car.

"I'm going to be really glad when we can hang out and not just sit and ask each other questions we don't have the answers to."

Maggie grinned.

"Are you telling me we're going to hang out when this is all done with?" she teased. It was half-hearted. Her nerves were starting to mount. They'd already told the sheriff where they were going and had a car in the area just in case they needed help. But still, they'd thought they had a hold on everything earlier that week...right before they'd been bulldozed in the middle of an intersection. Sarcasm and teasing were an easy way to distract at least some of that tension. Plus, Maggie couldn't deny there was some curiosity there, too. "What would you even talk to me about if you couldn't question my motives?"

Matt snorted and led the way to the front door.

"I'd probably just tell you that you talk too much." He grabbed the door handle and pulled. "Or finally just arrest you like I've always wanted."

His lips had pulled up into a dazzling smile. Maggie shouldn't have been surprised that her body seemed to take a moment to appreciate how good-looking the man was again. A warmth and longing started below her waist and moved across her body until the warning of an incoming blush made her move past the man inside. She hoped he hadn't read the excitement in her expression. They didn't have time for that.

Though Maggie was starting to come to the re-alization that she wouldn't mind making time for it later.

The lobby of Danny's Storage Facility wasn't as sterile as she thought it would be. Instead of the whites and gray and shine on the outside, there was more warmth and color inside. Framed pictures of family members and employees hung on the walls, comfortable-looking furniture and a silver-haired woman standing behind a desk with a generous smile, all contributed to the warmth that was clearly lack-ing on the outside.

"Good afternoon," she greeted. "Welcome to Danny's! How can I help you two?"

Matt didn't lead off by showing the kind woman his badge. Instead, he pulled out a smile that would make any woman's knees weak. Maggie was amazed the older woman was still standing by the time they were in front of her.

"Howdy," the detective greeted, amping up his Southern drawl. It was smooth and thick like peanut butter. Tasty. "I'm a detective with the Riker County Sheriff's Department. My name is Matt Walker and this is my associate." He motioned back to Maggie, omitting her name on purpose, no doubt.

The woman continued smiling and nodded to Maggie. If she recognized her, she didn't show it in her expression. Her focus zipped back to Matt.

"Nice to meet you two. How can I help you, Detective?"

"We heard about the break-in you reported this morning. We were wondering if you could tell us about that. We think it might be linked to a current case we're working."

The woman's expression pinched. She twisted up like she'd tasted something sour.

"It's the first time in ten years we've ever had something like this happen," she started, riled up in an instant. "Someone breaking in to our legacy units."

"Legacy units?" Matt asked.

"The units at the back of the facility that have been with us for years but have no one currently paying for them." Her look of anger turned momentarily sheepish. "I won't let my son Ralph empty any of them out. Some of those renters have been here since the beginning and, without them, we wouldn't have been able to get to where we are now."

A man walked out of the next room, cleaning his hands off with a paper towel. He shook his head but kept a smile on his face.

"Where we are now is my wife, Emily, putting in overtime to try to hunt down the owners of those units and telling them to pay up or lose their things. She's been glued to the phone and internet at the house for weeks, trying to find people." He walked up to Matt and nodded to them both. "A thankless job if I ever did hear one."

"And you must be Ralph," Matt guessed. The man nodded.

"They're here about the break-in," the woman explained. Just like that her earlier anger transferred to her son. He shook his head in disbelief.

"I guess it was only a matter of time before someone tried to break in, but it still gets my blood going," he said.

"Do you know what was taken?" Maggie jumped in.

Ralph must have really taken a good look at her then. His eyes stuck to the cuts healing across her face. No amount of lipstick could distract from them.

"To be honest, I don't know," he admitted. "We have thirteen legacy units and never kept stock of what was inside each. I wouldn't even have known anything was taken at all if all the locks hadn't been cut."

Maggie couldn't hide her surprise.

"Wait. *All* of the locks?"

Ralph nodded.

"All of the legacy units had their locks snapped off. With a bolt cutter, if I had to guess."

Well, that put a wrench in their theory. If Maggie had a key to one unit then why would she have needed to destroy all of the locks?

"And the report said you found them this morning but suspect it happened last week?" Matt asked, no hint of confusion in his expression. He was keeping a tight lid on his thoughts in front of the strangers.

"Since working on the renovations on the front of the facility, we rarely go to the back." Ralph motioned out the window that showed the tall fence. "We've added security cameras and a gate code to the front and haven't had any issues of break-ins or vandalism since. The most trouble we get is someone trying to let their friends follow them in without reentering their gate code. And even then that's not a big deal. The only reason I went back there was to help my wife try to track down the owners of the legacy units or their kin. Before today, the last time I had to go into those units was last Tuesday."

"That's—what—about eight days between now and then?" Matt asked. "Why do you think it was done Wednesday?"

The mother and son duo shared a look.

Embarrassment.

"Because that's when we found the hole in the fence."

MAGGIE COULD BARELY contain herself. She bounced from foot to foot next to Matt as they stood in front of the new portion of the storage facility's perimeter fence.

"We didn't make a police report because I was afraid it would hurt business." Ralph rubbed the back of his neck, clearly uncomfortable with the choice he had made. "When I did a pass-through to see if anyone was around, there was no one and I didn't notice the locks had been broken. To be honest I didn't look that hard at first in the back since no one goes there. Again, it wasn't until my wife sent me after the legacy units that I saw the locks." He sighed. "I made sure to include that in my statement today with the police. We also ordered more security cameras for the few weak spots we realized we had." Matt glanced over at Maggie. Her eyes were wide, taking in the now-repaired fence.

The one she said she would have never climbed to break in. The one she said she would cut a hole in instead.

"Can we go see the legacy units now?" Matt asked.

"Sure thing."

Ralph started to walk away but Matt held back

enough to grab Maggie's hand. She tore her eyes away from the fence.

"We still have questions," he said, voice low. "Not answers. Okay?"

It took her a second but then she nodded.

They followed Ralph. It wasn't lost on Matt that he held Maggie's hand longer than necessary. He also couldn't deny that if felt more right than he expected.

This case had been full of surprises, but Matt was starting to see it wasn't just the facts that were throwing him. It was Maggie herself.

Or, really, how he felt when she was around.

"This starts the lot of them," Ralph announced when they'd walked for a few minutes. It pulled Matt out of his head. "All legacy units are non-climate-controlled. The units on either side of the thirteen are empty. My brother is out getting new locks so, for now, they're open."

There were no clues outside the units that would lead them to any answers on why someone, possibly Maggie, would break all—or any, really—of the locks. The thirteen small units looked as normal as he would expect.

"Do you mind if we take a look inside them?"

Ralph shook his head.

"If these were normal units, I'd object, but seeing as no one has officially claimed them in years, have at it. Just please let me know if you want to take anything. Then we'll have to get into the details. I'm going to go check a few other empty units. Holler if you need me."

Ralph gave them space as Matt and Maggie started with the closest unit.

"Here we go," Matt said beneath his breath, becoming tense. Maggie gave him a quick smile. It actually helped.

HALF OF THE units were filled with boxes of odds and ends that had once meant something to someone. It felt eerie in a way to look at someone else's life, especially knowing that for whatever reason they hadn't come back to get or see about their things. Maggie tried to be respectful as they looked around each space, seeing if something jumped out at her. Nothing seemed disturbed and no memories surfaced for Maggie.

"Maybe this really wasn't you," Matt said when they were done looking in the eighth unit. "Maybe we've just been itching for a new lead so we fabricated this one."

He pulled an open box of trinkets closer to him. He peeked over the edge of the cardboard.

"There's too many coincidences," Maggie argued. She had to focus on not stomping out of the unit like some angry child. Her frustrations were starting to get the better of her.

Maybe Matt sensed that rising aggravation. He hung back as she went through the next unit. By the time she went to the twelfth, he had just gone into the tenth.

What if Matt was right?

What if they were creating more questions just because they couldn't find their answers?

It was a thought that almost cost Maggie the very thing she was looking for.

Unlike the other units, this one was less cluttered and more on the empty side. A few pieces of old furniture, a metal cabinet with a lock and boxes without labels lined the walls.

Maggie's attention zipped back to the lock. Her breath caught. It was the same type of lock that had been on the storage unit doors. But this one wasn't cut.

"Because you don't need to cut a lock when you have the key," she whispered to herself.

She took a step closer, trying to remember anything that would tell her what was in the cabinet, when a box next to it pulled her focus away.

And then trapped it.

"Oh, my God."

Maggie's heartbeat sped up like a racehorse out of the starting gate. Her hands nearly shook as she picked up the picture frame she couldn't take her eyes off or, rather, the picture in it.

"Did you say something?" Matt called out.

For the first time, Maggie felt like a fish out of water, gulping air while she tried to find the right words. At least the right way to say them.

They had finally found a lead. However, Maggie felt no joy in it. No excitement. Because, if she was right, there was a good chance that it was going to hurt the detective.

"Maggie?"

The concern in his voice only made her discovery that much more bittersweet, but she couldn't hide it forever.

"I did." She cleared her throat and spoke louder. "I found something."

Maggie turned toward the opening, ready to look at Matt Walker and tell him she was standing in his late wife's secret storage unit, when the calm breath she'd just claimed disappeared in a gasp.

Someone was standing in the walkway in front of the unit but it wasn't Matt. It wasn't even Ralph.

It was their mystery man.

He was smiling.

Though he could have been making faces and singing "Dixie," and Maggie wouldn't have cared. It was the gun he had pointed at her that made all the difference.

Chapter Seventeen

He was wearing clothes that were as average as they came, just as he had been the day he'd pummeled them with his truck. There were dark circles under his eyes and one heck of a bruise across his nose, but he seemed to be feeling better than they had been. Which probably meant he'd had his bullet wound in his shoulder doctored. He certainly didn't seem to have any issues holding the gun on her.

"Detective, I think it would be best if you put down your weapon. Or this time I'll do what the car crash didn't to Ms. Carson here."

Even though they were standing in two different storage units, concrete walls separating them, Maggie could imagine Matt's face as he realized their own personal nemesis was back. And had the upper hand again. The detective probably was as tense as she was, but sporting a more intimidating facial expression. Hard jaw, pursed lips, eyes a raging storm. While Maggie could barely keep the picture frame steady in her hands.

"I thought you said you don't kill women." Matt's voice was ice. The man's eyes stayed on him. The gun stayed on her.

"I did say that," he admitted. "But after the run-around this one has given me, I might reconsider if I don't get a win soon. So, please, drop your gun or I'll make sure her part in your investigating stops here."

Maggie wished the wall between them was gone. She wanted—no, *needed*—to see the detective. To know everything was going to be okay. To see those storm-cloud eyes and feel their power. Maybe it would make her feel less helpless. She glanced around the unit to see if there was anything she could use to defend herself. Or to attack.

"And what will you do with her if I follow your order?" Matt asked. "What stops you from shooting her now?"

The man actually grinned.

"Because I have a few questions only she can answer." His grin unhinged. His head tilted to the side like a dog hearing a foreign sound. Maggie didn't like the change. Or how fast it happened. "But you know, I can't really think of a reason for me to not shoot you."

Maggie took a small step forward. Her voice was louder than she thought was possible with the fear coursing through her.

"If you kill him then you'll not only have an entire county of law enforcement hunting you down, you'll have an entire *community* hunting you. And they won't stop until you're found."

The man glanced at her, the grin back. And just as sinister looking.

"You underestimate my power to disappear."

There was a clear point of pride in the way he said it. Maggie's stomach knotted.

"If you kill him," she started, slow but strong, "I'll fight until you have to kill me, too. Then I can't answer any of your questions."

The man didn't respond for a moment. Instead, he looked between them. Maggie wondered what Matt was thinking. Again, she wished the wall was gone.

"Oh, okay," he finally said. "I see. You two are a thing." He nodded in Matt's direction. "You're willing to die for her and she's willing to die for you. Looks like this investigation has been heating up while you two have been in hiding. How cute."

Maggie didn't have time to dwell on his words. All of his attention went back to Matt.

"So now we have another very real choice for you to make. You can put the gun down and let me take Ms. Carson here so we can have a little chat. Or you can not put it down and I'll just kill her and do what I do best and you'll never see me again or find out *any* truth whatsoever. Or, my new favorite option, I can just kill you now, which will force your girlfriend here to attack me until I kill her, too." The man laughed. "Now, if you ask me, the first option

is the best bet, considering it's the only one where
you both live. But I have to admit that while I might
have known your wife, I don't know you, Detective.
You might like having the women around you die."
His lips pulled into a wider smile. It was downright
sickening. "Everyone has their own secret kink after
all. Maybe that's yours. Who am I to judge?"

The world around them disappeared. All Maggie
could see and hear was a madman with a gun. It was
like she was seeing him for the first time. He wasn't
just a criminal, some unknown piece to a larger puzzle, he was the end game. Even without her memories, Maggie knew right then and there that she was
looking at pure evil. Smiling like he was at the damn
park or out with friends. Average looking in every
physical detail while hiding a core dripping with evil.
And she believed that evil.

Matt must have also believed it.

"Good choice, Detective," the man said, his eyes
moving downward for a moment. Maggie heard metal
hit concrete. He had dropped his gun. "Now, back up
against the wall, Detective."

"Why?" Matt asked, voice still arctic.

"Don't worry, I'm just going to shut you in. I think
it's time you took a time-out."

The man switched his aim from her to Matt and
stepped out of view. The moment she heard the sound
of the metal door shifting, Maggie made a split-
second decision.

She ran.

Fast.

Moving out of the twelfth storage unit, she ran like there was no tomorrow to the corner of the building, only a few units away. It gave her just enough time to clear the corner before the man yelled.

"Stop!"

But Maggie wasn't going to stop. She wasn't going to let him use her against the detective anymore. Instead she was going to use the adrenaline coursing through her, dulling the pain and wounds she'd racked up over the last two weeks, and try to put as much distance between herself and the man.

If he really wanted her, then he was going to have to catch her first.

THE DOOR SLAMMED DOWN, sounding like a gunshot in the new night Matt found himself in.

"Stop!" the man yelled on the other side. For a moment Matt thought the man was talking to him. Confused, he paused to listen. Footsteps raced away. Two sets.

She ran, Matt thought, adrenaline rocketing through every inch of his body within seconds. He scooped up his gun and grabbed the bottom of the door. If he knew he had a clean shot at their perp, he would have taken it through the door. Instead, he held the gun ready and pulled the door up.

It rose an inch and stopped. Matt fell against it, confused. He readjusted and tried again. It stopped again. Hung on something.

A lock.

Their mystery man had come prepared.

Matt took a few steps back. The unit was bathed in darkness but that hadn't stopped him from taking stock of its contents when he'd first come in. There was nothing he could use to push the door off its tracks.

Nothing but himself.

He squared his shoulders, held his gun low and charged forward. The pain that shot through his body as he hit the aged metal, mingling with the soreness that was already there, meant nothing to Matt. The only detail he was focused on was the fact the door was still standing.

He backed up to the middle of the room and tried again.

The metal and his shoulder protested in sound and pain.

"You can do this," he said.

He took his spot back up again. He dropped his shoulder low, ready again, when a sound chilled him to the bone.

A gunshot.

He stepped back until he was touching the wall. Matt wasn't about to waste another breath on being in the storage unit. He ran at the old metal door, mind already on the layout of the outdoor units they'd passed coming in. Because he had no plans on staying in the dark anymore. Not when Maggie was out there.

His shoulder connected with the door. This time it didn't stop. The metal overhead buckled and then snapped off the tracks holding the top of the door in place. Matt fell forward, riding the door as it fell beneath him. Together they hit the ground in a loud tangle of metal, human and dirt. It wasn't a perfect kicking-the-door-down move but it got him out in the daylight. He scrambled to his feet, rolling off the door and pulling up his gun. He took a beat to listen. No one made a sound.

Matt ran around the building, toward the front. Toward where he thought the gunshot had gone off. The small road between each row of outdoor units was covered in dirt. Matt moved fast across it, slowing at corners but keeping his eyes on the ground. Three buildings over and he finally saw what he was looking for. Footprints, small footprints.

Maggie.

He followed them past a row of units to around the building's corner. There he froze. Matt wasn't just looking at dirt anymore. There was blood, too. A lot of it.

"No! *Matt!*"

Like a string was attached from her voice to every part of his body, Matt was propelled around the corner. The man was there. He had Maggie's hair by the ends, yanking her out of an open unit. There was blood caking her shirt.

"I'm not playing around anymore," the man yelled. "You're going to tell me *everything*!"

Maggie stumbled to her knees. It only agitated him even further. He put the muzzle of his gun to her temple.

"Stop right there," Matt boomed. He closed as much distance as he could before the man's attention switched to him. Maybe the sorry son of a bitch knew that Matt wasn't going to let him off the hook as easily as he had before. His confidence appeared shaken when he finally locked eyes with Matt.

"Why can't you let me take her?" he asked. "I told you that *I won't kill a woman.*"

Matt planted his feet firm.

"But you said earlier you might," Matt reminded him. "And even if you won't, I bet you have friends who would." Matt took a tentative step forward. "I think it's time *you* put down the gun."

The man's focus scattered. He looked from Matt to his gun and then back to Matt. He was weighing his options. Judging by his widening eyes, he was realizing he didn't have many.

"If you take me in, you'll never know the truth about what happened to your wife," he said quickly. He shook his gun enough to make Maggie wince. Matt took another step forward in turn. "It's either her or the truth."

Matt didn't have to think about this choice. As much as he'd loved his wife, he'd accepted her death. He'd tried to move on. Just like she'd want him to do. And while he didn't want to lose the truth behind what had really happened, there was no way he was going to give up Maggie for it.

No, he would never sacrifice her.

Before Matt could let him know exactly what he thought about that choice, the man shook his head.

"Because I'm not going to jail, Detective," he said. "Not now. Not ever."

Matt believed him. So much so that his body reacted to the promise.

The promise of resistance.

When Matt spoke, he knew that one way or the other, it would be the last thing he said to the man.

"And she's not going with you."

The man's jaw hardened. His eyes narrowed. His brow creased. He swung his gun around, leaving Maggie in the clear, and tried to set his sights on his new target.

But Matt was faster.

His bullet found the man's chest.

It was all that was needed to take him down.

He hit the dirt. Hard.

Matt ran forward and kicked his gun away.

"Are you okay?" Matt asked, dropping down next to Maggie. Her eyes stayed on the man.

"He's trying to say something," she whispered.

Matt turned around. The man was looking at him, his mouth moving. They had to get closer to hear him.

"I t-told you," he whispered. "I—I don't kill women."

THE MAN DIED right then and there, in front of them both on the ground of Danny's Storage Facility. As far as last words went, his sounded movieworthy.

And unsettling.

Not that Maggie had the sanity to really think on them. The detective was back on her within seconds of the man's last breath.

"Where are you hurt?" he asked. "Maggie! Where are you hurt?"

He grabbed at her shirt, trying to find the source of the blood. It shifted the cloth and its wetness to a dry spot of her skin. The contrast shocked Maggie back into action.

"It's not mine," she said, voice barely registering even to her own ears. She cleared her throat.

"What?" Matt continued to search her body. She took his hands before rocking up to her feet.

"The blood isn't mine."

Maggie turned on her heel and stumbled into the open storage unit. Ralph was propped up against a wall, at the end of his own blood trail, barely conscious.

"He was coming to check on us when I ran into him. He tried to find us a hiding spot and got shot. I dragged him in here."

Maggie sat down on the concrete next to the man. She applied pressure to the stomach wound and ignored how warm his blood was as it pushed through her fingers.

"It's going to be okay," Matt assured over her shoulder.

Ralph was barely hanging on but managed to ask about his mom as Matt stepped out to call in reinforcements.

Maggie put on a smile she hoped conveyed un-yielding confidence.

"I'm sure she's fine. Just like you're going to be."

Maggie hoped she wasn't lying.

Chapter Eighteen

Ralph and his mother left in one ambulance together. She'd been ordered at gunpoint to open the gate but, thankfully, words were the extent of the gunman's attack. His focus had been resolutely on Maggie. And the contents of the locked cabinet. Neither of which he had been able to obtain in the end.

Maggie stood off to the side of the crime scene now being submerged in a constant wave of local PD and Riker County deputies. She watched as Matt was next to the gunman's body, talking to Detective Ansler. Without Matt she had no idea where she would be or if she'd even be alive. Their backup deputies had still been a few minutes out when Matt was finally able to call them in. That would have been a big enough gap for the man to take her away without anyone being able to follow.

The man might have said he never killed women, but the fact of the matter was that Erin Walker had been run over. As best as she could guess he had paid Ken Morrison to do it. In her book that meant he had no problem killing women, he just preferred outsourcing. Now with Ken and the man both dead Maggie was hoping for some peace. For all of them.

"How are you doing?" Maggie's heart jumped to her throat. Sheriff Billy Reed immediately looked apologetic. "Sorry, I thought you heard me walk up."

Maggie took a deep breath and let it out.

"It's okay. I was just stuck in my own head," she admitted. "But I'm doing okay. Though I wish we had more answers."

The sheriff nodded.

"But at least we know a man willing to kill is now off the streets," he pointed out. "Even if we don't have all of the answers, that's enough to make me happy."

Maggie didn't skip a beat.

"But I need more. *We* need more."

Together they looked over at Matt. He was talking to Detective Ansler. His face was stone.

"He hasn't gotten the chance to look in the unit you were in earlier, has he?"

Maggie's gaze stayed on the detective in question. He'd chosen her over finally knowing the truth about his wife, unaware Maggie had already stumbled upon a new lead.

"No. We were focused on Ralph until the ambulance got here and then you guys showed up."

The sheriff surprised her with a small sigh. She glanced up at him. He looked tired.

"So he doesn't know that the unit you were in belonged to Erin yet."

Maggie shook her head.

"No," she confirmed. "He doesn't."

They were quiet for a few seconds. Maggie was reminded that Sheriff Reed wasn't just Matt's boss, but also his friend.

"He's not going to take it well," he finally said. "But maybe what's inside will give us answers we couldn't get from him."

Maggie looked back at the gunman. Dead. She felt no sympathy for him. He'd shot Ralph without provocation *or* hesitation.

"Are you going to tell him?" She angled her entire body in front of the sheriff, no longer able to bear the sight of the man's lifeless body a few yards away.

"To be honest, I think it should be you who does it," the sheriff said. "I feel like it would mean more."

That confused her.

"Mean more?"

He fixed her with a pointed stare.

"You never believed Erin's death was simple and were criticized for it. Still, you pressed on until the road dead-ended. Years later and, even with more to lose than before, you still never gave up." He gave her a small smile. "Going down the roads you two went down to find the truth, in my book, makes you like partners. And hard news, good or bad, comes easier from partners."

Maggie returned the smile, touched by the sheriff's gentle words. She didn't have to ask it and he didn't have to say it but Maggie felt like he had just apologized and forgiven her in one fell swoop. Where the sheriff saw redemption, the others in Riker County's Sheriff Department would, too. Eventually.

It made Maggie's heart feel lighter.

Finally, she'd risen from the actions she regretted taking five years ago. Or, at least, how she'd handled the beginning of looking into Erin's death. She never should have cornered Matt the way she had. Especially after the funeral. There had been better ways to go about it but Maggie had been single-minded, driven by an obsession and pushed by unhappiness in her own life at the time. Maybe now she could reform her relationship with the department and the detective himself.

Though when she met Matt's gaze after he was done talking to Ansler, she felt the weight of a different burden settle.

She left the sheriff's side and moved closer to Matt.

"Did our mystery man have the key on him by chance?" she started.

Matt nodded. He produced the key she'd hidden at the bottom of the hotel pool from his back pocket. It looked impossibly small in the plastic evidence bag it was in.

"It was the only item he had on him aside from a key to a stolen car out front."

"Good." She took a breath. "Because I need to show you something."

Matt didn't question her as she led him back to the twelfth legacy unit. She paused only long enough to

Forgotten Pieces

look at the tenth's damage. The metal door was on the ground, bent awkwardly.

"Did you do that with your body?" she asked, surprised.

He nodded. No-nonsense.

"I had to get to you."

Maggie felt a butterfly dislodge in her stomach. It fluttered around, spreading warmth. She reached out and touched his hand.

But now wasn't the time to indulge in how Matt Walker made her feel.

Maggie left his side. She went for the picture frame she had dropped on the floor when she'd run earlier. Thankfully, it was still in one piece. She held it up to her chest but motioned to the locked cabinet.

"I think the key unlocks that."

Matt didn't need to be told twice. Still wearing the gloves Detective Ansler had given him, he pulled the key out and put it into the lock. It came undone without any issues. Maggie took a step closer.

They remained silent as he handed her a worn notebook while he pulled out a stack of pictures and newspaper articles. Separately they examined their pieces of evidence before Maggie finally understood.

Which made things even harder.

"She was investigating him."

Matt looked up from the picture in his hands. Maggie recognized their gunman in the top one, younger but definitely still him.

"Who?"

Maggie put the notebook down and gently took the photos from his hand. She then handed him the picture frame.

"Erin," she answered. "Matt, I think this is Erin's storage unit. Which means she was investigating the man… And I think that's why she was killed."

Maggie had never seen him look so confused before. It pained her to see a man like him, one built up on confidence that rarely failed, looking so lost. That expression only became more pronounced when he looked at the picture between his hands.

It was of a young woman dressed in a graduation robe and smiling for all she was worth. Maggie might not have known the woman but there was no denying that it was Erin in the picture.

Once more Maggie touched his hand.

Then she left him alone with his thoughts.

ERIN WALKER HADN'T trusted the new janitor who had started working at the hospital. His name was Seth and whatever their initial meeting was, it inspired suspicion in her. Enough that she began to dig deeper into who he was. Which led to the list of three names Maggie had found in the woman's locker five years ago.

Joseph Randall, Jeremy Pickens and Nathan Smith.

How she had gotten from Seth to those men, Maggie didn't know by reading her notebook alone. However, she did understand the thread that wove all four men together.

Erin Walker had suspected that, not only had the hospital's new janitor assumed each man's identity, but he'd also killed them to get it. Joseph had been in his early thirties, Jeremy had been in his midthirties and Nathan had been forty. Each man resembled the next and, now that Maggie had met Seth in person, she couldn't deny how similar he looked to those men.

In her notes, Erin called him the chameleon killer.

Finding men who looked like him and causing their deaths to look like accidents. As hers had.

A chill ran up Maggie's spine at the moniker.

However, there was nothing concrete that proved Erin's suspicions, which made Maggie wonder if Seth had already taken care of that evidence or if Erin had still been looking for some when she'd died. When he'd probably realized what she was doing. Then he'd found a felon, Ken Morrison, and managed to get him to take Erin out of the equation completely.

But what had brought him out of hiding after all these years?

Matt opened the door as if he could hear her thoughts.

"Ralph is in surgery but the doctors are very optimistic," he said. "His wife, Emily, was calm enough to answer a few of the sheriff's questions about the twelfth unit after promising to keep us updated on Ralph's condition."

Matt settled into the driver's side of the patrol car they had driven over in. Maggie had been seated in the passenger's side for half an hour as Matt, Detective

Ansler and Sheriff Reed had gone over every inch of the storage unit. He'd taken pictures of the pages in the notebook they'd found and given it to Maggie to look through while he finished up to see if she recognized or remembered anything. She hadn't. At least nothing they hadn't already figured out.

"The storage unit was under Erin's father's name," he started, turning over the engine and getting out of Park. Without the immediate danger of Seth he'd suggested they stop by her house to get cleaned up before picking Cody up from the hotel. Dried blood caked on her outfit wasn't the best accessory when greeting a young child. Or anyone, really. "Erin and her dad were never close and he passed away a few years before we got married. Almost everything in there is from when she was a kid with a few random pictures and memorabilia from her high school and college years thrown in. I don't think she used the unit often, if at all, except for what was in that locked cabinet." He navigated back to the main road and kept his eyes focused out the windshield. His jaw was tight. His entire body was tense. "After she passed away and the unit stopped being paid for, it fell into the legacy category. When Ralph's wife, Emily, started digging into who each of the units belonged to she couldn't remember Erin's name and called someone she thought might be able to help. Gabriel Thompson."

Maggie snapped her fingers.

"That's what changed," she exclaimed. "Gabriel owns the *Kipsy City Chronicle*, the newspaper I used to work for. He knows everyone in the city, heck, the entire county. His family has been here for generations. He must have known Erin's father. When he got to Erin's name he called me?"

Matt nodded.

"Detective Ansler just got off the phone with him. He said that Emily left a message about the unit, hoping to find someone. He knew your history with Erin. He thought it might help bring you some closure for a case that made you lose your reputation. His words." He looked pained. Apologetic.

"It's okay," she assured him. "I made the choices I made and that's that. We can't change the way we handled the past. I'm happy with who I am now."

Matt kept his eyes forward. His sharp expression didn't lessen.

"Gabriel thought it might win you some points in my book if you were the one who gave me the news of a forgotten storage unit that might have things I'd want of Erin's. That was Wednesday morning." His fingers tightened around the steering wheel, turning white. "If I'd only listened to you that morning, then…"

Maggie reached out and, for the third time that day, placed her hand on one of his. This time, though, she didn't let go. Instead, she moved it to the middle console and held it there.

"You got him now," she said softly. "That's all that matters. Okay?"

He glanced down at their hands and then her face. He let out a short breath and nodded.

Maggie didn't let go of his hand.

"But I do wish I had a better idea of everything I did that day. Like how did I get the key to the cabinet in the first place?" she asked. "And how did Seth hear about the storage unit anyway? Last Wednesday, without my memory, is still really confusing. Even if we know now that it started with a call from Gabriel, it doesn't explain why I broke into the storage facility, then took the key to the cabinet, went to a hotel room and hid the same key, and then at the end of the night, wound up at Dwayne Meyers's."

"That, I think I have a theory on," Matt said, coming to a stop at a red light. "Emily said a woman matching your description came in Wednesday morning and asked about the unit. You couldn't provide any ID showing you were related. They want to get rid of the legacy units but not without giving family who might be out there a fair shake first. She turned you away. So you took matters into your own hands and broke in." He gave her a sly smile. It was nice to see him smiling. Even though she'd had to break a law to get it. "The brand of lock that was used on the cabinet usually comes with a set of two identical keys."

"You think Erin left one of the keys *in* the storage unit."

Matt nodded.

"She didn't want me to know about the unit, so what better place to keep the copy safe?"

There wasn't any bitterness in the detective's tone but there was definitely a sadness there. A question. One he wanted to ask someone he couldn't. One Maggie couldn't answer.

While Erin's notes had given them answers, one she never wrote down was why she didn't tell her husband what she'd found. Maggie knew that question would weigh heavily on the man for a long, long time.

"So let's say I found the notes, decided to keep them in the unit because they've been safe there for years, and then what? I went back to my house then freaked out because Seth followed me? And who did I meet in the hotel?"

Maggie let out a long, long breath and dropped her head. It brought the blood on her blouse back into view. She let go of his hand. They didn't talk for a while.

Chapter Nineteen

Thanks to the Riker County Sheriff's Department, Maggie's front windows had been replaced and the inside of the living room cleaned. Matt looked out through the windshield and couldn't tell that anything had even happened. Let alone a madman had tried his best to scare Maggie away with the old brick-through-the-window trick.

Seth.

That had been his name. Or at least his current one. If what Erin had suspected was true—a fact that Detective Ansler had jumped on as soon as he'd shown him and the sheriff the contents of the cabinet—then Seth might have been the last man the chameleon killer had killed. And he had just been walking around pretending to be someone he wasn't.

Matt leaned back in the seat, making no move to get out of the car.

There was just something so surreal about feeling lost while knowing exactly where you were. Matt stared out the window but was now as blind as a bat to everything past the hood. Instead, he was cycling through memory after memory of his marriage.

Of Erin.

Looking beyond the pain of knowing she'd been intentionally killed to examining everything he thought he knew before any of that had ever happened. Trying to find the cracks in their marriage that he'd missed. The cracks his wife had fallen into while his attention had been on his job. The cracks that had created a cliff she'd been pushed off by a madman.

In hindsight it all made him feel like a fool.

And an even worse husband.

Why had she taken it upon herself to investigate Seth? Why not come to him?

"Matt."

Maggie's voice was becoming a normal part of his days, but the concern in the way she said his name was enough to break his trance. But not the lingering emotions attached.

He was mad, angry at himself and ashamed of what he hadn't seen all those years ago. What he hadn't done.

And what he had.

Looking into the green, green eyes of the woman who had fought harder than he had to solve his wife's murder. He'd been angry at her for such a long time and now he knew exactly why.

"Maggie, I was never really mad. Not at you."

Her eyebrow arched up in question.

"Back then, after Erin passed. I wasn't mad at you.

I was mad at myself. I thought of a thousand different scenarios of how I could have saved her had I done *something* different that day. But in none of them did I think I could have changed her fate. Changed her being there when she was. Changed what happened. And because of that, I felt helpless. I thought that maybe that meant she was supposed to die there regardless of anything I did or could have done. That it was fate." Matt felt the hole he'd pretended didn't exist start opening up. That darkness he'd tried to ignore for years.

"That's a kind of helplessness that destroys someone. One I knew I couldn't live with. So I tried to move on. I tried to put it all behind me. Pretended to accept that my wife had died alone on a sidewalk," he continued. "But then there you were, accusing me of having something to do with her death and then asking questions I should have been asking myself. And it made me mad. *Angry.* But it wasn't just at you, it was at myself, too." He paused, searching for the words he'd never said out loud. "I didn't want to listen to you then because I didn't think I could handle what it would do to me if you had been right. If her death hadn't been an accident. I've seen good men and women become obsessed, losing themselves in cases that, more often than not, lead nowhere. The closer you are to what's happened, the more you can't see the damage it does to you. To the soul. And I—I didn't want to lose what little I had left in my life, my job included. It grounded me. It gave me purpose when I didn't even want to get out of bed in the morning." He gave her the smallest of smiles, comforting himself by explaining it to her. To Maggie. To the woman who had been fearless at his side. "They say people grieve in different ways. Trying to pretend I had healed was mine."

Maggie's expression softened, but he wasn't done yet. What they'd found in that storage unit had shaken him. He needed to get it out.

"But how did I think I could be a good husband in death if I wasn't in life? How did I not know about everything we just found?" He hit the steering wheel, more anger spilling over. Or, really, self-loathing. "How could I have not known my *wife* was tracking a serial killer? How could I have missed that? Tell me, how does a good husband lose that much perspective about his partner that I wasn't even suspicious of what she was doing? Tell me, Maggie, how?"

Maggie answered by opening her car door and getting out. For a moment he thought she was going to leave him, go into the house, done with his outburst. But then, she curved around the hood and came up to his door, opening it wide.

"Step out," she ordered.

He listened, though there was hesitation.

Maggie reached out and took his hands in both of hers, planting herself firmly in front of him. Her face was open but hard. Stern. Then she spoke with words that were sharp, cutting and very clear.

"You want to know why you, the no-doubt good husband, didn't know what Erin was up to?" She squeezed his hands. He couldn't look away from her. He was locked in. "It's because your wife didn't want you to know," she said. "And so you didn't."

It was a simple explanation that, he realized now, compounded an entire side of his wife's life that he never knew existed. And somehow, the way Maggie said it, or maybe the way she looked at him now with those big, true green eyes, that it was enough of an explanation. Still, she sweetened the pot of her argument. Her words were softer but still just as clear.

"Wives. Husbands. Detectives. Reporters. We're all just people in the end. People who make decisions. Erin made them, I made them and now you have a decision to make."

"I do?"

She nodded.

"You can beat yourself up for the rest of your days, doubting yourself, or you can take a breath and move on. Happy with the fact that you helped get a crazy man off the streets." She smiled. "And saved a crazy woman in the process. More than once. Now, I'm going to go inside and clean up. Come in when you've made your decision."

Maggie didn't wait for his response. She took out her house keys and started to open the door.

Despite himself, Matt smiled.

"Erin would have liked you," he called.

Maggie paused in the doorway, long enough to respond.

"I think I would have liked her, too."

MAGGIE WAS FEELING GOOD.

While they didn't have all the details, they'd still managed to stop Seth. She had the utmost confidence the sheriff's department could fill in any holes that remained. Eventually. Until then she was relieved that the target was off her, and her son's, backs, grateful to be able to help finish Erin's investigation, and happy that the detective had finally opened up to her. However, that feeling of everything starting to look up didn't last past her shower.

She sat down on her bed, wrapped in a towel, and caught a glimpse of the blouse she'd stripped out of on the floor. The dark crimson that stained most of it was dry but she still felt its wetness against her skin. She looked down at her hands, remembering how Ralph's blood had covered them. How he'd cried out when she pressed down on the wound. How he'd been barely hanging on to consciousness and still made sure to ask about his mother, worried she'd been hurt.

Maggie slapped a hand over her mouth as a cry escaped her throat. Her vision blurred. She thought about the car crash, the way Matt hadn't moved, lying against crushed metal and broken glass, and how Seth had dragged her away with no idea what would happen next.

Then all Maggie could think about was the blood on Seth's chest—and his lifeless body.

Maggie hung her head, burying her face in her hands.

The weight of everything had finally become too heavy. No amount of humor or sarcasm could hold it back.

Another sob racked her body; tears began to drench her hands; images she wished she could forget filled her mind.

She didn't even hear when Matt called out to her from the other side of the door. This was her breakdown. This was the price she had to pay to process the danger and fear she'd experienced in the past two weeks.

"It's okay. Let it out."

The bed next to her sank lower.

Maggie didn't look up as two strong arms wrapped around her. She felt embarrassed. Dealing with danger and death was part of Matt's job. She bet he'd never broken down. Not like this.

That embarrassment escalated as Matt turned her into his chest. Yet it somehow felt right. He just was there.

What felt like hours, but had to be only minutes, went by. Maggie slowly disentangled from the man. She hung her head and used her towel to wipe at her face. If there had been a mirror in front of them she was sure she wouldn't like her reflection. Swollen, red eyes plus cuts and bruising from the past week without an inch of makeup to lessen the marks.

"Sorry," she tried, voice cracking. Maggie cleared her throat and tried again. "It just finally caught up to me. Everything, you know?"

"I know."

Matt pulled away. It made her exposed skin, not covered by the towel, feel cold. Maggie looked up, not liking the contrast in feeling. Matt's gaze was already on her. His eyes locked within hers.

Suddenly, Maggie was acutely aware of several things.

Matt wasn't just *close*, he was touching her. His jeans rubbed against her bare thigh where the towel had ridden up. Which made the fact that the only thing keeping all of her from all of him was the cloth of her towel and the thin fabric of his clothes. Then there was the heat. Beneath her skin yet crawling over every inch. All within seconds. Starting below her waist and yet seemingly always there. Maggie couldn't help herself. Her eyes traveled down to his lips.

The world around them quieted to an impossibly loud silence.

"Maggie."

Her name had never sounded so good. Or different. All her life she'd heard it. From her mother, her teachers and colleagues, friends and even her ex-husband. But the way Matt pronounced those two syllables in that moment was like hearing it for the first time.

Her chest started to rise and fall faster. It was like the air in the room had gone. Or maybe she was just trying to breathe in something else.

Someone else.

She met those eyes, those blue, blue eyes, and

knew she was on the brink of everything changing. That nothing would be the same if she could just...

"Maggie." His voice was filled with grit.

It wasn't him repeating himself. No, it was different. It felt different. Like he was fighting her. Fighting himself. Fighting something.

He moved his hand, slow and precise, up to the side of her face. The tips of his fingers skimmed her jaw, his thumb brushing along her cheek. She leaned into his palm until his fingers found the back of her neck, his thumb stopping beneath her ear. He rubbed against her skin in an excruciatingly slow circle.

Maggie felt like she had just run a marathon. Her breath becoming harder to catch after every second that passed. She bit her lip to keep from trying to fill the silence. If remaining quiet prolonged Matt Walker touching her the way he was—*looking* at her the way he was—then she'd gladly never say another word.

Though she wasn't the one who broke that silence.

Matt leaned in, just as slow as his hand had cupped her cheek, until their foreheads were touching. She stayed locked in his gaze, his eyes never leaving hers for even a second, and almost moaned as his hand slid back across her cheek. This time his fingers tucked beneath her chin. His thumb, however, had its own agenda. It ran across her top lip, stopping at the edge until she let go of her bottom. She parted her lips as he traced both of them.

How could she ever breathe after this?

"Maggie?"

She heard the question. It was the reason she allowed herself to answer.

"Yes?"

She barely heard her own voice.

"Thank you."

Maggie was almost completely submerged in desire for the man touching her that she nearly decided to just accept his words, no questions asked. But desire, lust and even something stronger than the two—deeper than the two—aside, Maggie was still Maggie. Curious to the ends of the earth. She had to know why, out of everything he could have and could not have said, he chose *those* two words.

"What for?" she whispered.

He licked his lips. When he spoke Maggie felt pleasure in every part of who she was.

"For waking me up."

His lips turned up into a smile that she knew was real.

Then he wasn't smiling anymore.

He was kissing her.

And God, it felt good.

Maggie moaned as his lips went hard and fast against hers. No longer was it time to take things slow.

They both turned into each other. She let Matt take the lead. His hands went from her neck to her hair to pushing her gently onto her back. She'd been so focused on pulling him closer Maggie forgot about the very towel she'd been so aware of minutes ago.

It parted like the Red Sea as she moved. Cold air pressed against her exposed breasts.

Matt broke the kiss and gave her a look she could only describe as unsure. It was endearing. So much so that Maggie found herself smiling.

"What?" he asked, propped up on his elbows, inches away from her bare skin.

Maggie couldn't help but laugh.

"It's just unfair." She glanced down at herself. "I showed you mine…"

That look of uncertainty the detective had been harboring evolved into a mischievousness she had always guessed was beneath his intense, cop-like surface. His lips quirked up into a smirk that simply smoldered. He dropped down, ran his lips against hers and then sat up.

"So it's only fair I show you mine, right?"

It was a question but he was already answering it. His boots thudded to the floor and his shirt found its way across the room. Maggie's heartbeat galloped at the sight of the man over her. Like a statue. She saw no flaws in him.

When he got to the button of his jeans, Maggie reached out and grabbed his hand.

"Let me help with that one, Detective."

Matt's eyes widened and then that smirk heated up.

"Yes, ma'am."

Chapter Twenty

Matt hadn't expected to kiss Maggie Carson. He wasn't going to lie, the thought had crossed his mind, but he hadn't thought he'd act on it. At least not *that* day. He hadn't even thought he would go inside her bedroom.

But then he'd heard her cry out.

Nothing could have stopped him from trying to comfort her—to ease the jarring reality she'd witnessed in the past few days—some way. Somehow.

Kissing her?

Not what he had expected.

Not that he was complaining.

Lying naked in Maggie Carson's bed, arms wrapped around the equally naked Maggie Carson herself, and there was no bad feelings for what they'd just done. And definitely no denying how good the two of them had been at the choice they'd just made.

"Well, that wasn't how I expected to get Matt Walker in my bed."

Matt chuckled into her hair.

"You always have to say something, don't you?"

Maggie moved her head back to look at him. He liked how good it felt having his arm hang over her hip, protective, with her bare skin against his.

"These are two things we've already said," she pointed out, grinning. "Does that mean we're beginning to be predictable?"

Matt couldn't help but laugh again.

"I think what we just did was anything but predictable."

She shrugged. Matt felt the movement against his body.

"Does that make it a good thing?" she asked.

"It definitely doesn't make it a bad thing."

Maggie smiled. She opened her mouth to say something else when Matt's phone started to go off. They shared a look.

"I'm putting my money on that being the sheriff," she said, moving out from under his arm. "Which means I'm going to step into the bathroom while you take that call."

Maggie slipped into the bathroom while Matt dashed across the room to his jeans. A wild, giddy feeling took over him. Like he was a teenager caught doing something he wasn't supposed to be doing. It made him smile. The first genuine smile he'd had in a long time. One that grew when he saw the call *was* from the sheriff.

"What's up, Billy?"

The sheriff didn't waste any time.

"I know I told you to take some time to get things back to normal…" Matt glanced at the bathroom door he'd just watched a naked Maggie run through. He didn't know if their being together was what Billy meant when he'd said *normal*. "But I thought this might help. All three of our cars are back in working order thanks to two very hardworking and fast mechanics in Kipsy."

"So the Bronco lives?" Matt asked, his day getting even better. Everyone knew that the Bronco had been Billy's late father's personal car and that Billy had loved his father dearly.

"Oh, ye of little faith," the sheriff responded with a laugh. "You can't kill the Bronco that easily."

"Glad to hear it!"

Matt moved around the room, collecting and putting his clothes on while getting into the more serious details of what happened next. Billy still insisted that Matt take a few days off to really rest, and his last task would be to bring Maggie to the hotel where both of their cars were being delivered.

"You're probably ready to sleep back in your own bed instead of being cooped up in a hotel," Billy commented before they ended the call. Matt agreed but didn't feel the relief he thought he would. While hotel living had never been on his to-do list, he had to admit he'd gotten used to seeing Maggie and Cody throughout the day. Eating with them, walking around with Cody and watching a game show or two with Maggie after Cody had fallen asleep.

The case might have been dangerous but it had also been an excuse. One that forced them together.

One that they didn't have anymore.

Matt finished dressing and relayed what the sheriff had said as the two of them made their way back to the car. If Maggie had any concerns about leaving the hotel for good, she didn't voice them. Instead, she kept the conversation light. She answered Matt's question about her job and, by the time he was parking outside the hotel, they were talking about a camping trip Cody's school was taking in a few months. Neither spoke of what they'd done, or what it meant for them now.

It didn't bother Matt. Not at first. He took one last walk with Cody around the hotel while Maggie packed their things. Then he threw his belongings in his bag and thanked Caleb again. But when he was standing in the parking lot, in front of both of their cars, Matt didn't like how final it felt.

"Well, Detective, I guess it's time to go," she said, twirling her keys in her hand.

Matt nodded.

"I guess it is."

The two of them stood there, quiet for a moment. Matt was reminded again of feeling like a teenager. This time an awkward one.

"All right, well, I'll see you later, then," Maggie said, finally breaking the silence. "Stay safe, Detective."

She gave him a small nod and turned away.

Matt watched her go.

But couldn't let her leave.

"Hey, Maggie?" he called.

She paused in the doorway of her car.

"Yeah?"

"I promised Cody that I'd still go exploring with him after all of this was over," he said. "And Billy says there's this park near here that has some really good trails." He smiled. "Maybe we can explore them sometime. You know, the three of us."

Cody was the one who answered.

"Yeah! Say yes, Mom," he yelled through the open door.

Maggie laughed.

"Well, I'd hate to make you break your promise." She flashed him a smile. It was warm. "I guess I really will see you later, Matt."

"Yes, ma'am."

He watched as she drove off and then did the same.

It wasn't until he was out of the shower in his own house that his phone rang again. This time he didn't recognize the number.

"Hello?"

"Hi, is this Detective Walker?" It was a woman's voice, one he recognized but couldn't place.

"This is he."

"I don't know if you remember me but my name is Kortnie Bean. I'm a nurse at the Kipsy ER."

Matt pictured the red-haired woman with ease.

"The nurse who talked with Maggie *both* times we were there," he filled in.

"Yeah, that's me! And she's actually why I'm calling."

Matt's body tensed; his back straightened.

"What's wrong?" he asked, already eyeing his shoes across the room.

"Oh! No! Nothing," she replied. "At least I don't think so. See, I just worked on a man who came in with a gunshot wound and his mother mentioned that Maggie was with him when he was shot. She said she thought Maggie was okay but, well, with her track record, I thought I'd check in. I know you two have been together a lot and assumed you'd know for sure if she *was* okay."

Matt's body loosened.

"That's nice of you," he said, honest. "I'm sure Maggie will appreciate it, too. But yeah, she's fine. A little shaken up but this time no injuries."

"Good! I didn't like the routine the three of us were making in here," she said with a laugh.

"I'm right there with you, but that should be over with now. Hopefully no more hospital visits for a long time."

"So I'm assuming that means y'all caught your perp. That's great," she exclaimed. "That plus your friend waking up, and you must be on cloud nine right about now."

Matt paused.

"My friend?"

"Yeah, the man you rode in with last week? The one who was assaulted along with Maggie?"

"He's up?"

Matt grabbed his shoes.

"Yeah. A few hours ago! I heard he was lucid as could be. It's a miracle, really!"

Matt couldn't help but smile.

"This day just keeps getting better."

"KEEP LOOKING!"

Maggie dived into the cushions while Cody got on his stomach to look underneath the couch.

"I see it," he yelled. "I can't reach it!"

Maggie dropped to her stomach, moving through the new soreness that made her think of the detective—no matter how pleasant it was—and extended her arm until her fingers wrapped around the cordless phone. While she preferred her cell phone, her mother had always made the point that landlines still came in handy. Which was true, considering Maggie hadn't been able to replace her lost cell phone yet.

"Carson residence," she answered, rolling onto her back. She trapped Cody beneath her in the process. He erupted in giggles.

"Hey, Maggie, this is Dwayne Meyers."

Maggie sat up, excited.

"Oh, my God, Dwayne! How are you? I had no idea you'd woken up!"

The man chuckled. It sounded familiar and foreign all at the same time. Years ago she'd asked the then detective about any connections he might know between Erin and Ken Morrison. He'd been nicer than most of the people she'd talked to but still, she hadn't been friends with the man. The last time she remembered talking to him had been in passing at a local football game. Then again, they knew for a fact she'd been at his house the week before. She'd been afraid she wouldn't get the chance to ask him why.

"I've actually been up since yesterday but the doctors didn't want to say anything until they had a better handle on my condition."

"And how is your condition?"

"Right as rain," he said, smile clear in his voice. "Just a little bruised and sore but nothing sleeping in my own bed won't cure."

That caught Maggie off guard.

"Wait? They're letting you go?" She wasn't a doctor but she doubted letting a patient who had been in a coma go home one day after he woke up was the best move.

"I'm actually already at home." He continued before she could express her concern. "To be honest, it took some pretty intense persuasion but at the end of the day the doctor admitted I was in good condition. He called it a miracle."

Maggie nodded to herself.

"It sure sounds like it," she admitted. "Have you talked to Matt already? I know he was really worried about you."

"I did. In fact that's why I called. The sheriff told me about what happened, you know, with your memory and I'm officially offering to fill in the blanks for you."

Maggie's heartbeat started to speed up.

"The blanks? You mean why I was at your house that night?"

"Not only that but before we got attacked, you told me everything. Everything you did that day."

Relief and excitement mixed together into an intoxicating cocktail. She turned and gave Cody a wide smile. He returned it.

"That's wonderful!"

"But if you wouldn't mind, I think it would be easier if we did this in person," he said. "I already got Matt and the sheriff on the way over. Do you mind coming out here?"

Maggie nodded profusely, already standing.

"I'd love that!" She held her hand out to Cody and then pulled him up. "I might be a bit, though. I need to get a sitter for my son."

Again she heard Dwayne's smile through the phone.

"I'm okay if you bring him out here," he said. "I have cable to entertain him while we all talk."

"Sounds great! We'll leave now!"

Maggie ended the call and looked at her son.

"Where are we going, Mom?" he asked.

"We're finally going to get the rest of the answers."

MAGGIE AND CODY sang to the radio all the way to Dwayne's. Neither knew all the words to any of the songs and, if she was being honest, they both could use some lessons. However, Maggie was finally feeling a weight lift at the realization she'd know what she'd done the week before. It made her happy. A feeling she was already experiencing thanks to a certain detective. Cody must have picked up on her mood. He mimicked the excitement all the way until she cut the engine outside Dwayne's house.

"Now, you make sure you behave while we're here," she said, helping him out and holding his hand. "We have some adult stuff to talk about that's important to me and Matt and the sheriff."

"Matt's going to be here?"

Maggie didn't miss the extra infusion of excitement at the mention of his name. Another point of endearment for the man she'd finally opened herself up to.

"Yes, sir! It looks like we beat him, though, so you're going to have to entertain yourself with the TV while I talk to Mr. Meyers, okay?"

"Kinda like I'm on a case?"

Maggie laughed. There was no mystery where that talk had come from. Or who.

"Yeah, kind of like you're on a case."

Cody nodded, serious. But then he lowered his voice.

"Who is Mr. Meyers?"

Maggie opened the screened-in porch's door. She

dropped Cody's hand to keep it from falling over. Someone had knocked it off its hinges.

Seth.

It reminded her that while she wanted answers, she'd forgotten the shape that Dwayne must have been in. How he looked. And how that might scare her son.

Maggie paused before knocking on the front door. She bent down and looked Cody in the eyes.

"I want you to know that Mr. Meyers might not look that great right now," she started, trying to choose her words carefully. "He got hurt recently and probably has a lot of bruises and cuts, but he's okay now. He just looks worse than he is."

Cody's innocent eyes widened.

"How did he get hurt?"

Maggie had always tried to tell the truth to her son and so she made no exception here.

"A bad man was angry at him."

"And he hurt him?"

"Yes, but the bad man is gone now. He won't hurt him or anyone else again. Okay?"

Cody nodded. Maggie kissed his forehead and stood tall again. She ruffled his hair and turned toward the front door.

"But why did he hurt him?" Cody asked.

Maggie froze, fist in midair.

"What?"

"Why did the bad man hurt Mr. Meyers?" he repeated.

Maggie opened her mouth but no answer came out. She didn't have one.

Why *had* Seth beaten Dwayne?

She knew that Seth didn't kill women but why hadn't he killed Dwayne? Beating him to a pulp with a bat still riled up local law enforcement so why hadn't he just finished the job?

And why had she been at Dwayne's to begin with?

A sinking, sick feeling began to fill her stomach.

Maggie took a step back from the door as the one lone detail from the week before filtered in. It wasn't a memory but it was a fact.

"Oh, God."

Maggie grabbed Cody's hand again and spun around. She pulled him along with her so hard that he stumbled. She didn't have time to explain to him why they were leaving when they'd just gotten there.

They just needed to leave.

Now.

Because Maggie knew without a doubt that Seth hadn't used the bat on Dwayne.

She had.

Which meant they hadn't been invited over for the truth. He'd invited her over to silence it. And she'd been stupid enough to fall for it and, worse, bring her son.

Maggie fumbled with her keys, her hands already shaking from the new dose of adrenaline raging through her.

But for the third time in one week, someone had a different plan for her.

She heard the footsteps too late.

The last thing she remembered before everything went black was Cody screaming.

Chapter Twenty-One

Light.

Bright, blinding light.

Maggie tried to blink it away. When that didn't work she tried to bring her hand up to shield her eyes. The movement almost made her sick. Not only from pain but from fear.

Because she couldn't move much at all and she couldn't understand why.

"And here I thought you weren't going to wake up."

Maggie blinked again until her focus finally adjusted. She was sitting on a bed, legs stretched out in front of her. She could move them but barely. Duct tape was wrapped around them, making her feel like she was in a cocoon. Her hands weren't better off. The unmistakable coldness of cuffs pressed against her wrists.

Those details alone would have put her in a panic but the way Dwayne Meyers was smiling at her, sitting in a chair in the corner, turned her body to ice.

"Where's Cody?" she rasped out.

How long had she been unconscious?

"Don't worry, he's in the guest bedroom watching TV. It was the only thing that would stop him from whining." There was such disgust in his words that Maggie panicked.

"Cody?" she yelled out. "Cody?"

"Mom!"

It was faint but he was definitely in the house.

"Are you hurt?" she asked, looking away from Dwayne's obvious annoyance.

"No," Cody answered. "I'm scared!"

Maggie's heart threatened to break in half at his words.

"Everything's going to be okay," she tried.

Dwayne let out a too-loud sigh. He leaned forward so his elbows rested on his knees.

"Now tell him if he doesn't keep quiet, I'm going to kill you in front of him," he said. "You don't have to say that verbatim but I suggest you run that point home." His words were less words and more of a hiss. A dark, evil hiss. One Maggie believed.

"Hey, little dude, I'm going to need you to be really quiet right now," Maggie said. Her voice wavered but she powered through. "So don't say anything else until I come in there, okay?"

"Okay," he answered. It was small. Scared.

The cold that permeated Maggie's body heated in anger at the sound. She turned her gaze back to the man who held the forgotten pieces of her memory.

She'd seen the pictures of Dwayne on the floor,

bloody and unconscious, but it was nothing like sitting in front of the real thing. Bruises, dark and bright and varying shades between, covered his face, arms and neck. His nose had been broken and sat at an odd angle. He was still in pain. A lot of it.

That much she could tell for certain.

Which only added to the anger he seemed to have for her.

"You're admiring your handiwork right now, aren't you?" he asked, motioning to his face. The bruises there were the darkest. "You sure caught me by surprise when you decided to use me as batting practice. I didn't expect you to have any fight in you past your sarcastic comments."

Maggie took a small breath, trying to calm her racing heart. She needed to stay focused. Stay alert.

"I don't remember doing it," she said. "I don't remember last Wednesday at all."

The man snorted. Even that small bit of movement seemed to hurt him.

"That's what I heard. Apparently, Seth hit you a little too hard." He smiled. If you could even call it that. "Or not hard enough, if you ask me. The damned fool always did have a soft spot for women. I heard what happened to him, too. Can't say I'm sorry about it. Just another no-good killer off the streets."

That earned a few words from Maggie.

"And what are you?" she asked. "Are you a killer, Dwayne?"

He eased back in his chair, his smile sharpening.

"You really *don't* remember anything, do you?"

He didn't wait for her to answer. "You couldn't let the truth go and then it let you go. How much fun is that?" He repositioned himself again, like he was trying to get comfortable. Maggie couldn't imagine that he could, given his injuries.

The injuries *she* had inflicted on him.

"You know you're a lot like her in that respect," he continued. "Erin, I mean. She also couldn't stop digging—couldn't let the truth go—and look where that got her. Dead on the side of the road."

"It was you," Maggie guessed. Dwayne didn't just have the missing piece, he *was* the missing piece. "Erin saw you in the truck before you went after her. She was waving at you."

Dwayne laughed. It was crude and cold and felt wrong in every fiber of her body to even hear.

"Which is what you figured out last week," he said. "In fact, we've already had this conversation. So let me skip ahead to answer a few more of your questions. It was me who was driving Ken's truck that night. It was me who ran her over. And it was me who framed drugged-out-of-his-mind Ken. Then I just walked away."

Maggie couldn't stop a small gasp from coming out. Picturing Erin's body lying in the street like some forgotten rag doll. He talked about killing her like she had been nothing more than a piece of debris that had fallen out of some truck's bed. And then he'd just walked away.

"You didn't look so surprised the last time I told

you this," he continued. "But I guess this time you found a different set of clues. To be honest, I thought I'd gotten rid of all of Erin's evidence into Seth."

"So she figured out you were helping Seth, tried to take you both down, and you killed her for it."

"Oh, on the contrary, I didn't even know who Seth was until Erin came along."

"I don't understand."

Dwayne's smirk was back in full force.

"Erin was a very *singular* woman. She had this sixth sense about people. I swear, if you had a secret, she could sniff it out just from a few minutes of talking to you. So when Seth started working at the hospital, she started to suspect he wasn't who he said he was. It probably didn't help that he was a grade-A idiot when it came to keeping all of his identities in order. I mean, sure, the first two times he was okay but by the time he became Seth he was having some issues keeping all his lies straight." He shrugged, dismissive. Like it was no big deal he was talking about a serial killer taking people's lives and then *living* them. "Either way Erin asked to meet me one night in private. Matt was in the middle of helping with some stressful cases at the department, the kind that kept him up all night, and was strung out and sliced thin, and she said she didn't want to add to his stress until she had proof. Concrete proof. She was like that. Always worried about people worrying but also unable to let go of things she had no business grabbing in the first place. So she told me what she knew about the man and I told her I'd look into it."

Dwayne paused and cracked his neck. Although his tone was calm, Maggie could feel the mounting anger behind his words.

"And I did. I looked into it and went straight to the source. I cornered that weasel after one of his shifts and asked him everything I could. And by God if he didn't crack. Laid out the whole truth right at my feet." He chuckled. "I remember thinking, 'How can this guy, this little idiot of a man, pull off what he's been pulling off for almost a decade?' So I asked him. You couldn't find a more surprised man than me in that room all those years ago when he started talking about how he'd been living off his old identities' accounts, sucking them dry and then moving on." He rubbed the stubble on his chin. "He even showed me on his phone all the money he had earned being Seth. The man was nearly a self-made millionaire just by hacking and killing nobodies." Dwayne's nostrils flared. His lips thinned. His smirk long gone. He tapped his chest with his index finger. "When I'd been breaking my back for the department for years and barely getting by?" He shook his head. "No. Not me. Not anymore. Not then, not now, not ever again."

"He bribed you to keep quiet," Maggie whispered. She felt sick.

"No, ma'am," he was quick to respond. "I *took* what I was due from someone who found a way around the system. He didn't fight me and I didn't rat him out. We had an understanding."

"The only problem was Erin."

Maggie hated saying the words but knew them to be true. The reason she'd lost her life hadn't just been Seth's self-preservation. It had also been because of Dwayne's greed.

"She hadn't told anyone else and I already had what I thought was all of the evidence she'd collected. Plus, Seth was too weak to shut her up. So I did what had to be done." His anger ebbed. Maggie's stomach rolled when she recognized pride starting to bolster the man up. "I waited a few months, making sure *you* stayed in your lane and didn't find anything out, and then I retired. Easy as pie."

"How could you do that to Matt?" Maggie had to ask. "He looked up to you and still does. You're his mentor. His friend. How could you hurt him like that?"

"Listen, I still care about that boy," he said, hands up in defense. "Hell, I'm even going to feel bad about what I'm sure I'm going to have to do to him when I'm done with you, but back then? I wasn't about to let his nosy wife stop me from taking an opportunity I sorely deserved."

Maggie listened to every word he said but was still stuck on one part.

When I'm done with you.

It made the fear and anger in her chest turn to panic. Not for her but for her son.

And for Matt.

"He'll come for you. Matt will. He'll come for me and my son." Tears started to prick the edges of Maggie's eyes. Still, she persevered. "And when he comes, he'll bring hell to your doorstep for what you've done."

Dwayne didn't waste a breath.

He smiled.

"I'm counting on it."

MATT WASN'T SEEING RED. He was seeing blood.

After his call with Kortnie he'd barely made it out of his driveway before another call had come in. It hadn't been a good one. Apparently, Dwayne hadn't just woken up. He'd left the hospital, but not until he'd shot two people and killed a cop in the process.

Matt had called Maggie before he'd even processed the shock of the news. When she hadn't answered, he'd called in Deputy Carrington, who lived across the street from Maggie.

She wasn't home.

The house was empty.

Matt realized then that he already knew where she might be. Dwayne had played them. Something Matt guessed Maggie had figured out before she'd lost her memory. Which meant that Dwayne either thought he had a loose end to take care of before he bolted, or he wanted something else. Something more simplistic.

Revenge.

Matt slammed his hands against the steering wheel.

He couldn't pretend to know or guess at Dwayne Meyers's state of mind anymore. The man had been his mentor. That mentor had just shot a civilian and then killed a good cop. Which meant he was more than capable of killing a good woman.

And probably already had.

Erin.

Matt took a deep breath, trying to keep his rage under wraps. It was a hard feat, considering the car he saw parked behind Dwayne's house as he pulled up. It was Maggie's.

Suddenly everything felt different. *Looked* different. The house he'd once found comfort in at times when he needed a friend was now dark. Filled with an evil Matt had been too blind to see.

He cut the lights and stopped the Jimmy out far enough that it couldn't be seen from the front windows. He pulled out his phone and texted Billy that Maggie was there.

That she was with Dwayne.

A man neither of them knew anymore.

Matt pulled out his gun and checked the clip. His phone started to ring before he could open his door. It was Billy and Matt knew what he'd say if he answered.

Wait for us.

But Matt wasn't going to do that.

Instead, he left his car as quietly as he could and moved across the lawn, ready for anything.

The screen door on the patio was still broken. It

would make noise if he moved it to get to the door.
He knew Dwayne wasn't one to lock his windows,
so he used that fact to his advantage. Slowly yet as
quickly as he could, Matt went to the first window.

The living room looked the same as it had the
week before when he'd first found Dwayne and Maggie unconscious. Neither were there now. He continued moving along the house until he was at the small
bathroom window. With the foundation already raised
a foot, he had to rise up on the tips of his toes to see
inside. It, too, was empty. Next was the guest bedroom. It was small. Matt doubted if he was holding
Maggie that he'd do it in there. Still, with the mind-
set of no stone going unturned, he looked in through
a part in the blinds.

Fresh rage nearly compelled Matt to fling the window open.

Cody was sitting on the bed, hands and legs bound.
The TV in the corner was on. Maggie wasn't with
him. Neither was Dwayne.

Matt knew that it might have been the wiser of
choices to keep looking to see where Dwayne was.
However, one look at Cody, small and with duct tape
on his skin, and nothing could have made him leave.
He only prayed the window was unlocked.

Chapter Twenty-Two

"I still don't understand what led me back here last week."

Dwayne stood, tall and proud despite his pain. Threats of Matt and the rest of the department swarming in had fallen on deaf ears. Though his distaste for what he was about to say was clear. His frown was deep as he explained.

"You found Erin's secret stash and started poking around Seth. He can kill people no problem, but the man gets jumpy when cornered. You asked a few too many questions and he went squirrelly. So he tried to convince you that Erin did suspect him but had it wrong all those years ago. He told you not to worry because I'd already questioned and cleared him before Erin's death."

"Which I knew was a lie," Maggie said.

He nodded.

"But you didn't suspect my involvement then. You just thought it was a piece of the mystery you'd somehow missed. I told you we needed to meet in person to get all the details ironed out. You weren't happy about my meeting place but you didn't argue, either." That's why Maggie wound up at the hotel. That's who she had been meeting.

"Why not shut me up while we were there? Why let me go?"

Dwayne cracked his neck again. Like he was gearing up for something. Maggie hoped she wouldn't have to find out what.

"You might not have suspected me but you didn't fully trust me, either," he said. "You kept talking about Erin's notes but refused to tell me where they were. I remembered how annoyingly determined you were when it all first happened so I couldn't take the chance that you had stashed it somewhere that might bite me in the ass down the line. I tried to convince you that you needed to tell me everything—to *show* me everything—but, in hindsight, I guess I pushed too hard. You got all weird, went to get food from the lobby and then came back with some excuse about having to leave. So I let you."

"Did you come to my house after that?"

Maggie still wanted to know why she'd left in such a hurry.

He shook his head.

"That would be the idiot. He tried to take a crack at *persuading* you to take him to what you'd found. You left. From there you disappeared for a few hours. So I came back here." His grin was back. "And who do I find snooping around my house? You didn't find any proof I was involved but, man, did you have a mouth on you." He shrugged. "A man can only take so much."

"That's when I attacked you," she filled in. "It *was* in self-defense."

A muscle in his jaw twitched.

"I should have shot you the moment I saw you," he growled.

Maggie knew it was only a matter of time before Dwayne was done entertaining her. In fact, she couldn't think of any reason why he was explaining everything that had happened to her in the first place.

"So what's the plan?" she decided to go ahead and ask. If they were getting to the end of his mental rope, then she wanted to prepare herself for what was coming. It was the only way she could try to think of a plan to get Cody out unharmed. The thought of him being hurt by the deranged man in front of her was too much. She couldn't let that happen. She *wouldn't*.

"My plan? It's simple." He reached into the back of his jeans and pulled out a gun. Maggie froze. She hadn't seen the weapon at all. "I'm going to kill you like I killed Erin. And then? I'm going to show Matt exactly what it feels like to have everything ruined. And then I'm going to kill him, too."

Dwayne lifted the gun, but before Maggie could scream, a shot rang out.

The man she guessed she would see in her nightmares for years to come, toppled over onto the bed. Maggie was stunned for a moment, confused as to why she wasn't the one who had fallen. It wasn't until she tore her eyes away from the dead body of Dwayne Meyers that she noticed the man standing in the hallway behind him.

Through the open door, Matt lowered his gun.

"I promise I didn't wait until he was done talking and then shot him for dramatic effect," he said. "It just took me longer than I expected to get Cody out of the house."

"He's okay?" Maggie rushed.

"Yeah, he's locked in my car. I wasn't sure how this would all shake out and didn't want him to be in any danger."

Maggie opened her mouth to thank him but all that came out was a sob.

Matt didn't waste any time taking her out of the bedroom. He found Dwayne's handcuff keys and unlocked them from her wrists. The moment Maggie's hands were free she threw her arms around the detective's neck and kissed him for all she was worth. He returned the favor in kind. They didn't speak while he cut the tape off her legs next. The moment they were free Maggie let them lead her outside and right up to Matt's car.

To say she cried the moment Cody was in her arms, unharmed, was an understatement.

To say her heart expanded to the brink of almost bursting when Matt put his arms around both of them, promising mother and child everything was going to be okay, was another giant understatement.

Together, the three of them sat in the back seat of his car and waited for first responders. It wasn't until the sheriff arrived that Matt left their side.

And even then he wasn't gone long at all.

MAGGIE SHOULDN'T HAVE been surprised when Kortnie met them at the ER doors. She might not have known Maggie that well but when she pulled her in for a hug, Maggie felt like they were old friends. The nurse looked exhausted and drained but still managed a joke.

"I think we might just need to get you a helmet," she said, walking them straight back to a room.

Maggie was surprised when Matt joined in.

"Don't worry. I've already thought about it."

He gave Maggie a small smile.

She might have been tired, too, but seeing him smile gave her enough energy to be grateful. She mussed Cody's hair. A lot of things could have gone wrong that day. If Matt hadn't come…

Maggie didn't want to think about what *could* have happened. Instead, she went through the now-familiar routine of making sure her third blow to the head hadn't left any permanent damage. Thankfully, it hadn't. Though the doctor insisted she stay the night for observation. She wouldn't admit it but the idea didn't offend her. Cody had fallen asleep on the bed next to her and she wasn't far behind.

The only thing keeping her from giving in to the abyss of sleep was the need to talk to Matt. The sheriff had taken him outside to talk. It wasn't until a half hour later that he reappeared. He smiled. It was tired, but there. He took the chair beside her and glanced at the TV in the corner before starting.

"They found a note in the desk at Dwayne's," he said, voice low. "He never planned on trying to run. After he realized we were looking into Seth together and actually getting somewhere, Dwayne wanted me to pay for everything. For not stopping Erin or you back then and for not stopping you now. That was his final stand. He didn't write much else but I assume he would have tried to kill anyone who came. Even if it wasn't me who got there first." Maggie reached out and took his hand but he continued before she could try to comfort him. "You know, I thought about feeling guilty for a minute. About not being able to stop Erin or you, not being able to do what you two did instead and keeping you both out of danger." The corners of his lips turned up ever so slightly. "But the fact of the matter is I'm damned proud of you both."

Maggie returned the smile.

"And I'm sure Erin would be proud of you, too," she said. "Because I know I am."

A quiet moment passed between them. It stretched past their bruises, cuts and the damage that couldn't be fully measured or seen. They had been broken but had survived. Together. Now it was time for them to start to heal.

Maggie patted the spot next to her on the bed. Matt didn't question it. He slid in next to her, packing them in the hospital bed like sardines in a can. But it wasn't uncomfortable.

In fact, it felt just right.

TWO MONTHS LATER and the twisted web that Dwayne Meyers and Seth Armstrong—whose real identity was now being looked into by the FBI—had woven had finally been mostly unraveled. The city of Kipsy and Riker County as a whole knew to thank Erin and Maggie for finding out the truth. Something that meant a great deal to the loved ones of Seth's known victims. Two of the families drove out to give their personal thanks while the rest wrote letters or called. Maggie handled each encounter with grace, telling them that Erin was the true hero of the story, not her.

But Matt and the rest of the Riker County Sheriff's Department didn't see it as one-sided. Billy made it known throughout the department and county that any old grievances they'd had with Maggie had been misplaced and were absolutely over. She even received a job offer back at the *Kipsy City Chronicle*, which she ended up turning down. The idea of finally going forward with writing her true crime novel had taken hold of her and wasn't letting go. Matt had already started helping her with research. It only made sense. They were, after all, spending most of their free time together. Although Matt knew, even without the excuse of work, being with her and Cody was just where he wanted to be. Period.

They'd fallen into their own little routine. One that felt right. One that felt whole.

While he never in a million years would have guessed Maggie Carson could make him feel that way, Matt couldn't deny that it had happened. It wasn't until one Saturday, after finishing exploring a trail with Cody and returning to the house, that he was able to finally put words to what he now had.

A team.

* * * * *

Look for the next book in Tyler Anne Snell's
THE PROTECTORS OF RIKER COUNTY
miniseries,
LOVING BABY,
available next month.

And don't miss the previous books in
THE PROTECTORS OF RIKER COUNTY
series:

SMALL-TOWN FACE-OFF
THE DEPUTY'S WITNESS

Available now from Harlequin Intrigue!

THE LIGHT WAS in her eyes, blinding her. Macey Night couldn't see past that too-bright light. She was strapped onto the operating room table, but it wasn't the straps that held her immobile.

He'd drugged her.

"I could stare into your eyes forever." His rumbling voice came from behind the light. "So unusual, but then, you realize just how special you are, right, *Dr. Night*?"

She couldn't talk. He'd gagged her. They were in the basement of the hospital, in a wing that hadn't been used for years. Or at least, she'd thought it hadn't been used. She'd been wrong. About so many things.

"Red hair is always rare, but to find a redhead with heterochromia... It's like I hit the jackpot."

A tear leaked from her eye.

"Don't worry. I've made sure that you will feel everything that happens to you. I just—well, the drugs were to make sure that you wouldn't fight back. That's all. Not to impair the experience for you.

Fighting back just ruins everything. I know what I'm talking about, believe me." He sighed. "I had a few patients early on—they were special like you. Well, not *quite* like you, but I think you get the idea. They fought and things got messy."

A whimper sounded behind her gag because he'd just taken his scalpel and cut her on the left arm, a long, slow slice from her inner wrist all the way up to her elbow.

"How was that?" he asked her. His voice was low, deep.

Nausea rolled in her stomach. Nausea from fear, from the drugs, from the absolute horror of realizing she'd been working with a monster and she hadn't even realized it. Day in and day out, he'd been at her side. She'd even thought about dating him. Thought about having *sex* with him. After all, Daniel Haddox was the most respected doctor at the hospital. At thirty-five, he'd already made a name for himself. He was *the* best surgeon at Hartford General Hospital, everyone said so.

He was also, apparently, a sadistic serial killer.

And she was his current victim.

All because I have two different-colored eyes. Two fucking different colors.

"I'll start slowly, just so you know what's going to happen." He'd moved around the table, going to her right side now. "I keep my slices light at first. I like to see how the patient reacts to the pain stimulus."

I'm not a patient! Nothing is wrong with me! Stop! Stop!

But he'd sliced her again. A mirror image of the wound he'd given her before, a slice on her right arm that began at her inner wrist and slid all the way up to her elbow.

"Later, the slices will get deeper. I have a gift with the scalpel, haven't you heard?" He laughed—it was a laugh that she knew too many women had found arousing. Dr. Haddox was attractive, with black hair and gleaming blue eyes. He had perfect white teeth, and the kind of easy, good-looking features that only aged well.

Doesn't matter what he looks like on the outside. He's a monster.

"Every time I work on a patient, I wonder…what is it like without the anesthesia?"

Sick freak.

"But not just any patient works for me. I need the special ones." He moved toward her face and she knew he was going to slice her again. He lifted the scalpel and pressed it to her cheek.

The fingers on her right hand jerked.

Wait—did I do that? Had her hand jerked just because of some reflex or were the drugs wearing off? He'd drugged her when she'd first walked into the basement with him. Then he'd undressed her, put her on the operating table and strapped her down. But before he could touch her any more, he'd been called away. The guy had gotten a text and rushed off—to surgery. To save a patient. She wasn't even sure how long he'd been gone. She'd been trapped on that operating table, staring up at the bright light the whole time he'd been gone. In her mind, she'd been screaming again and again for help that never came.

"You and I are going to have so much fun, and those beautiful eyes of yours will show me everything that you feel." He paused. "I'll be taking those eyes before I'm done."

Her right hand moved again. *She'd* made it move. The drugs he'd given her were wearing off. *His* mistake. She often responded in unusual ways to medicine. Hell, that was one of the reasons she'd gone into medicine in the first place. When she was six, she'd almost died after taking an over-the-counter children's pain medication. Her body processed medicines differently. She'd wanted to know why. Wanted to know how to predict who would have adverse reactions after she'd gone into cardiac arrest from a simple aspirin.

It's not just my eyes that are different. I'm different.

But her mother...her mother had been the main reason for her drive to enter the field of medicine. Macey had been forced to watch—helplessly—as cancer destroyed her beautiful mother. She'd wanted to make a change after her mother's death. She'd wanted to help people.

I never wanted to die like this!

But now she could move her left hand. Daniel wasn't paying any attention to her fingers, though.

He was holding that scalpel right beneath her eye and staring down at her. She couldn't see his face. He was just a blur of dots—courtesy of that bright light.

She twisted her right hand and caught the edge of the strap. She began to slide her hand loose.

"The eyes will be last," he told her as if he'd just come to some major decision. "I've got to explore every inch of you to see why you're different. It's for the good of science. It's *always* for the good. For the betterment of mankind, a few have to suffer." He made a faint *hmm* sound. "Though I wonder about you…about us. With your mind…maybe…maybe we could have worked together."

And maybe he was insane. No, there wasn't any *maybe* about that. She'd gotten her right hand free, and her left was working diligently on the strap. Her legs were still secured, so she wasn't going to be able to just jump off the table. Macey wasn't even sure if her legs would hold her. The drug was still in her body, but it was fading fast.

"But you aren't like that, are you, Dr. Night?" Now his voice had turned hard. "I watched you. Followed you. Kept my gaze on you when you thought no one was looking."

She'd felt hunted for days, for weeks, but she'd tried to tell herself she was just being silly. She worked a lot, and the stress of the job had been making her imagine things. She was in her final few weeks of residency work, and everyone knew those hours were killer.

Only in her case, they literally were.

"You don't get that we can't always save every patient. Sometimes, the patients die and it is a learning experience for everyone."

Bullshit. He was just trying to justify his insanity.

"You see things in black and white. They're not like that, though. The world is full of gray." He moved the scalpel away from her cheek...only to slice into her shoulder. "And red. Lots and lots of red—"

She grabbed the scalpel from him. Because he wasn't expecting her attack, she ripped it right from his fingers, and then she shoved it into his chest as deep and as hard as she could.

Daniel staggered back. Macey shot up, then nearly fell off the table because her legs were still strapped and her body was shaking. She yanked at the straps, jerking frantically against them as she heard him moaning on the floor.

The straps gave way. She sprang off the table and immediately collapsed. She fell onto Daniel—and the weight of her body drove the scalpel even deeper into him.

"You...bitch..."

"You bastard," she whispered right back. Then she was heaving off him. Her blood was dripping from her wounds and she crawled to the door. He grabbed her ankle, but she kicked back, slamming her foot into his face, and Macey heard the satisfying crunch as she broke his nose.

He wasn't so perfect any longer.

"Macey!"

She yanked open the door. Her legs felt stronger. Or maybe adrenaline was just making her stronger. She ran out of the small room and down the hallway. He was going to come after her. She knew it. She needed help. She needed it *fast*. There were no security monitors on that hallway. No cameras to watch her. No help for her.

Her breath heaved out and her blood splattered onto the floor. She didn't look back, too terrified that she'd see Daniel closing in on her. The elevator was up ahead. She hit the button, smearing it with her blood. She waited and waited and—

Ding. The doors slid open. She fell inside and whipped around.

Daniel was coming after her. He still had the scalpel in his chest. *Because he's a freaking doctor. He knows that if he pulls it out, he's done. He'll have massive blood loss right away. But the longer that scalpel stays in...*

It gave him the chance to come for her.

His lips were twisted in a snarl as he lunged for the doors.

She slapped the button to close the elevator, again and again and again, and the doors *closed*.

Macey was shaking, crying, bleeding. But she'd gotten away. The elevator began to move. Gentle instrumental music filled the air.

The doors opened again, spitting her out on the lobby level. She heard the din of voices, phones ringing and a baby crying somewhere in the distance. She walked out of the elevator, naked and bloody.

Silence. Everything just stopped as she staggered down the corridor.

"H-help me..."

A wide-eyed nurse rose from the check-in desk. "Dr. Night?"

Macey looked down at her bloody body. *"H-help me..."*

"I'VE FOUND HIM." Macey Night exhaled slowly as she faced her team at the FBI headquarters in Washington, DC. All eyes were on her, and she knew just how important this meeting was. She'd spent five years hunting, searching, never giving up, and now, finally... "I believe that I know the location of Daniel Haddox." She cleared her throat and let her gaze drift around the conference room table. "Daniel...the serial killer otherwise known as 'The Doctor' thanks to the media."

A low whistle came from her right—from FBI special agent Bowen Murphy. "I thought he was dead."

Macey had wanted him to be dead. "I never believed that he died from his injuries. That was just a story that circulated in the news. Daniel was the best surgeon I ever met. He knew how to survive."

"And how to vanish," said Samantha Dark. Samantha Dark was in charge of their team. The group had been her brainchild. Samantha had hand selected every member of their unit. The FBI didn't have official profilers—actually, "profiler" wasn't even a title that they used. Instead, Samantha and her team were called "behavioral analysis experts." But the people in that conference room were different from the BAU members who worked typical cases in the violent crimes division.

Each person in that small conference room—each person there—had an intimate connection to a serial killer.

Her gaze slid over her team members.

Samantha Dark…so fragile in appearance with her pale skin, dark hair and delicate build, but so strong inside. Samantha's lover had been a killer, but she had brought him down. She'd been the one to realize that personal connections to serial perpetrators weren't a weakness…they could be a strength.

Tucker Frost. The FBI agent's bright blue stare held Macey's. Tucker's brother had been a serial killer. The infamous Iceman who'd taken too many victims in New Orleans. His exploits were legendary—scary stories that children whispered late at night.

Her hands fisted as her gaze slid to the next member of their team. Bowen Murphy. His blond hair was disheveled, and his dark gaze was intense as it rested upon her. Bowen had hunted down a serial killer, a man who the local authorities had sworn didn't exist. But Bowen had known the perp was out there. A civilian, he'd gone on the hunt and killed the monster in the shadows.

And then...then there was Macey herself. She'd worked side by side with a serial killer. She'd been his victim. She'd been the only "patient" to escape his care alive.

Now she'd found him. After five years of always looking over her shoulder and wondering if he'd come for her again. She'd. Found. Him. "You're right, Samantha," Macey acknowledged with a tilt of her head. "Daniel Haddox *did* know how to vanish." Her voice was quiet. Flat. "But I knew he wouldn't turn away from medicine. I knew he would have to return to his patients. He would *have* to pick up a scalpel again." But there had been so many places he could have gone. He could have easily stayed under the radar, opening up a clinic that dealt only in cash. One that didn't have any government oversight because it wasn't legitimate. One that catered to the poorest of communities.

Where he would have even greater control over his victims.

"I also knew that he wouldn't stop killing," Macey said. Once more, her gaze slid back to Bowen. She often found herself doing that—looking to Bowen. She wasn't even sure why, not really. They'd been partners on a few cases, but...

His gaze held hers. Bowen looked angry. That was odd. Bowen usually controlled his emotions so well. It was often hard to figure out just what the guy was truly thinking. He would present a relaxed, casual front to the world, but beneath the surface, he could be boiling with intensity.

"Why didn't you tell me that you were hunting him?" Bowen's words were rough, rumbling. He had a deep voice, strong, and she sucked in a breath as she realized that his anger was fully directed at *her*.

"The Doctor isn't an active case for our group," Macey said. They had more than enough current crimes to keep them busy. "We have other killers that we have been hunting and I didn't want to distract from—"

"Bullshit." His voice had turned into a rasp. "You forgot you were on a team, Macey. What impacts you impacts us all."

She licked her lips. He was right. Her news *did* impact them all. "That's why I called this meeting. Why I am talking to you all now." Even though her instincts had screamed for her to act. For her to race up to the small town of Hiddlewood, North Carolina, and confront the man she believed to be Daniel Haddox. But… "I want backup on this case." Because the dark truth was that Macey didn't trust herself to face Daniel alone.

Samantha's fingers tapped on the table. "How can you be so sure you've found him?"

Macey fumbled a bit and hit her laptop. Immediately, her files projected onto the screen to the right. "This victim was discovered twenty-four hours ago." Her words came a little too fast, so she sucked in another breath, trying to slow herself down. "A victim who is currently in the Hiddlewood ME's office. The autopsy hasn't even begun, but the medical examiner was struck by what she felt was a ritualistic pattern on the victim." She licked her lips. "Look at the victim's arms. The slices, from wrist to elbow. The Doctor always made those marks first on his victims. Those are his test wounds. He makes them to be sure his victims can feel the pain of their injuries, but still not fight him."

Silence. Macey clasped her hands together. "We got lucky on this one because we have a medical examiner who pays close attention to detail—and who seems very familiar with the work of Daniel Haddox. Dr. Sofia Lopez sent those files to the FBI, and I've got…I've got a friend here who knows what I've been looking for in terms of victim pathology." When she'd seen those wounds, Macey had known she'd found the bastard who'd tormented her. "I think the man who killed this victim is Daniel Haddox, and I think we need to get a team up to Hiddlewood right away."

Tucker leaned forward, narrowing his eyes as he stared at the screen. "You think this perp will kill again? You're so sure we're not dealing with some copycat who just heard about Daniel Haddox's crimes and thought he could imitate the murders?" Tucker pressed.

No, she wasn't sure. How could she be? "I think we need to get up there." Her hands twisted in front of her. She wasn't supposed to let cases get personal,

Macey knew that, but…how could this case *not* be personal? Haddox had marked her, literally. He'd changed her whole life. She'd left medicine. She'd joined the FBI. She'd hunted killers because…

Because deep down, I'm always hunting him. The one who got away. The one I have to stop.

Samantha stared at her in silence for a moment. A far too long moment. Macey realized she was holding her breath. And then—

"Get on a plane and get up there," Samantha directed curtly. Then she pointed to Bowen. "You, too, Bowen. I want you and Macey working together on this one. Get up there, take a look at the crime scene, and…" Her gaze cut back to Macey. "You work with the ME. If Daniel Haddox really committed this homicide, then you'll know. You know his work better than anyone."

Because she still carried his "work" on her body. And in her mind. In the dark chambers that she fought so hard to keep closed.

But now I've found you, Daniel. You won't get away again.

Tucker rose and came around the table toward her as she fumbled with her laptop. "Macey…" His voice was pitched low so that only she could hear him. "Are you sure you want to be the one going after him? Believe me on this…sometimes confronting the demons from your past doesn't free you. It just pulls you deeper into the darkness."

Her hands stilled on her laptop. She looked into Tucker's eyes and saw the sympathy that filled his stare. If anyone would know about darkness, it would be Tucker. She lifted her chin, hoping she looked confident. "I want to put this particular darkness in a cell and make sure he *never* gets out."

He nodded, but the heaviness never left his expression. "If you and Bowen hit trouble, call in the rest of the team, got it? We always watch out for each other."

Yes, they did.

She put her laptop into her bag. Tucker filed out of the room, but Samantha lingered near the doorway. Bowen wasn't anywhere to be seen. Macey figured that he must have slipped away while she was talking to Tucker. Clutching her bag, she headed toward Samantha.

"How many victims do you think he's claimed?" Samantha's voice was quiet as she asked the question that haunted Macey.

Every single night...when she wondered where Daniel was...when she wondered if he had another patient trapped on his table. *How many?* "We know he killed five patients before he took me." They'd found their remains in that hospital, hidden behind a makeshift wall in the basement. Daniel had made his own crypt for those poor people. He'd killed them, and then he'd sealed them away.

"He's been missing for several years," Macey continued. Her heart drummed too fast in her chest.

"And serial killers don't just stop, not cold turkey." Samantha tilted her head as she studied Macey. "He might have experienced a cooling-off period, but he wouldn't have been able to give up committing the murders. He would have needed the rush that he got when he took a life."

How many victims? "I don't know how many," Macey whispered. And, because she trusted Samantha, because Samantha was more than just her boss—she was her friend—Macey said, "I'm afraid to find out."

Because every one of those victims would be on *her*. After all, Macey was the one who hadn't stopped him. She'd run away from him, so terrified, and when she'd fled, he'd escaped.

And lived to kill another day.

Samantha's hand rose and she squeezed Macey's shoulder. "You didn't hurt those people—*none* of those people."

"I ran away." She licked her lips.

"You survived. You were a victim then. That's what you were supposed to do—*survive*."

She wasn't a victim any longer. "I'm an FBI agent now."

"Yes." Samantha held her gaze. "And he won't get away again."

No, he damn well wouldn't.

After a quick planning talk with Samantha, Macey slipped into the hallway and hurried toward her small office. As always, their floor was busy, a hum of activity, and she could hear the rise and fall of voices in the background. She kept her head down and soon she was in her office, shutting that door behind her—

"I would have helped you."

Macey sucked in a sharp breath. Bowen stood next to the sole window in the small room, his gaze on the city below. His hands were clasped behind his back, and she could see the bulk of his weapon and holster beneath the suit jacket he wore.

She put her laptop down on the desk. "Samantha said we should be ready to fly in an hour. She's giving us the FBI's jet to use—"

He turned toward her. "Do you trust me, Mace?"

Mace. That was the nickname he'd adopted for her, and half the time, she wasn't even sure that he realized he was changing her name. But…it was softer when he said "Mace" and not "Macey." For some reason, she usually felt good when he used that nickname.

She didn't feel good right then. *Do you trust me?* Was that a trick question? She frowned at him. "You're my partner. I have to trust you." Or else they'd both be screwed. She was supposed to watch his back, and he was supposed to watch hers. It was pretty much the only way the FBI worked.

He crossed his arms over his chest as he considered her. "I have to ask… What will happen if you come face-to-face with Daniel Haddox?"

She stared up at him, but for a moment, she didn't

see Bowen. She saw Daniel. Smiling. His eyes gleaming. And a scalpel in his hand. The scalpel was covered in her blood.

Don't miss
INTO THE NIGHT.
Available December 2017 wherever
HQN Books and ebooks are sold.

www.Harlequin.com

Get 2 Free Books,
Plus 2 Free Gifts—
just for trying the Reader Service!

SPECIAL EXCERPT FROM

⊕ HARLEQUIN®

I N T R I G U E

*Sarah Hampton knows that the recent murder of an old
friend is linked to a terrifying night they experienced
back in high school, and war-hardened Tyler Grant is
the only one who knows the danger they're in...*

*Read on for a sneak preview of
OUT OF THE DARKNESS
by Heather Graham*

Tyler watched as she walked into the parlor. Sarah.
Whom he hadn't seen in a decade. She hadn't changed
at all. Yet she had changed incredibly. There was nothing
of the child left to her. Her facial lines had sharpened
into beautiful detail. She had matured naturally and
beautifully; all the little soft edges of extreme youth had
fallen away to leave an elegantly cast blue-eyed beauty
there as if a picture had come into sharp focus. She was
wearing her hair at shoulder length; it had darkened a
little into a deep, sun-touched honey color.

He stood. She was staring at him in turn.

Seeing what kind of a difference the years had made.

"Hey," he said softly.

They were both awkward, to say the least. She started
to move forward quickly—the natural inclination to hug
someone you held dear and hadn't seen in a long time.

He did the same.

She stopped.

He stopped.

Then they both smiled and laughed, and she stepped forward into his arms.

Holding her again, he knew why nothing else had ever worked for him. He'd met so many women—many of them bright, beautiful and wonderful—yet nothing had ever become more than brief moments of enjoyment, of gentle caring. Never this…connection.

He had to remember she had only called on him because their friend had been killed, and he was the only one who could really understand just what it was like.

They drew apart. It felt as if the clean scent of her shampoo and the delicate, haunting allure of her fragrance lingered, a sweet and poignant memory all around him.

"You came," she said. "Thanks. I know this is crazy, but…Hannah. To have survived what happened that October, and then…have this happen. I understand you're some kind of law enforcement now."

"No. Private investigator. That's why I'm not so sure how I can really be of any help here."

"Private investigators get to—investigate, right?" Sarah asked.

When the horror of their past is resurrected,
can Tyler keep Sarah safe from a killer set on
finishing what he started?

OUT OF THE DARKNESS *by* New York Times
bestselling author Heather Graham.

Available January 16, 2018 from
Harlequin® Intrigue.

www.Harlequin.com

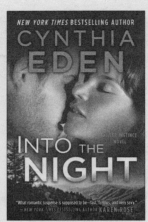